# MOVIN

# MOVING FORWARD

Abiola Awolola

**To order additional copies of this book, contact:**
Xlibris LLC
0-800-056-3182
www.xlibrispublishing.co.uk
Orders@xlibrispublishing.co.uk
521116

# CONTENTS

'What a very courageous and confident writing approach. There is definitely something "lovely" and "fragrant" about this book' (Sola Oladipo, Yes Minister).

# DEDICATION

All praise goes to God Almighty for His faithfulness.

This book is dedicated to my four lovely angels—namely, Itunu, Taiwo, Kehinde, and Oluyomi.

The book is also dedicated to my parents, Pastor and Deaconess (Mrs) Awolola, and also to Pastor Johnson Sulade Adeniji.

Abiola Oluyemi Awolola is a Management Accountant by profession and a member of the Associate of the Chartered Association of Certified Accountants (ACCA).

She is also a gospel singer; her debut album is titled Your Name is great. She is an award winner of Praise Tek Gospel Music Award 2013 (PGMA).

She is blessed with four lovely children namely Itunu-Oluwa, Taiwo, Kehinde and Oluwayomi.

# PROLOGUE

'YOU COMPROMISED AND got married to this man. Traces of this attitude were apparent at the time of your courtship, but you compromised and got married to him,' Pa James alleged.

'You are a believer. Why did you get yoked with the world? Didn't you know that a woman cannot change a man? What you see is what you get. You either wait until he becomes a believer before you date him, or you run completely away from such a relationship.'

'You are very correct, sir. He is not a believer,' she replied slowly. 'I hopefully thought I could change him once we get married. I was lost in love.'

Pa James's sociable voice began to turn gruff. 'That wasn't love, it was lust of the flesh. Teniola, you followed the flesh, you were not brought up that way.'

# CHAPTER 1

# Open Eyes

P A JAMES NODDED off whilst praying for Phebean and her daughter, Teniola. Phebean and Tenny (as Teniola was fondly called) travelled from Lagos to Gbongan to see Pa James. Tenny was on a visit to Nigeria, which was a sharp contrast to New York, where she lived with her husband, Robert.

Tenny bore a striking resemblance to her beautiful mother, with a well-shaped nose, rounded dark face complemented with locks of finely knitted black hair. She was often called Black Ebony because of her exquisiteness.

She urgently wanted to speak with Pa James; she wanted him to pray for her. She travelled to the motherland to find solace in the arms of her family and a soothing word from the servant of God, her grandfather, Pa James. She wanted Pa James to wake up and listen to her sobbing, to her distress. As she and her mum sat in silence waiting for Pa James to come out of his 'sleep trance', she cast her mind back to the heart-destroying trauma and non-stop physical battering that had been haunting her.

'Mum, he will soon wake up?' It sounded more like a statement.

Phebean paused and studied the significant-looking Pa James in a manner suggesting that she was used to his sudden trance to the unknown world. Pa James would commonly start a prayer and, after a couple of minutes, sink into silence, his eyes totally shut. He sometimes accompanied his abstraction with a snore!

Phebean was Pa James's niece. She was brought up in the village by Pa James and his family after the demise of her parents. She moved to the city after getting married to Dave, Teniola's father. Phebean made it a habit to visit Pa James, most especially on spiritual matters.

Pa James was a prophet, a devoted Christian, but he was never an overseer of a church. All his prophecies had always come to pass.

Nevertheless, it was difficult to fathom why a gifted man like Pa James would doze off in the middle of his prayers. This sleep trance could take up to ten minutes before he opened his eyes. Phebean was used to this drama, but Teniola was yet to figure it out.

'How long do we have to wait for? Can't we wake him up?' Teniola further asked.

Phebean shrugged. 'Five to ten minutes,' she responded, having spent a decade of her lifetime with Pa James and his family and knowing well how long it could take him to open his eyes. 'And we can't wake him up. If we do, in no time, he will doze off into another round of sleep.'

Unexpectedly, the distinct friendly voice Phebean knew so well was heard; it was the sociable tone of Pa James. 'I just saw your father . . .' Pa James at long last spoke in his well-articulated and rich Yoruba-Oyo dialect, both eyes still closed.

Phebean gave a heavy shrug and then shook her head in disapproval before responding to Pa James's statement. 'I've told you not to say such things again, my father died thirty years ago!' she exclaimed.

Pa James laughed, finally opening his one functioning eye, which now gazed at the Constant Apostolic Church almanac which hung on his living room wall.

'The whole street was white like the snow we see on TV. Have you seen snow before?' Pa James asked, looking at Teniola.

'Yes, Baba. Snow falls in America, where I live,' Teniola responded.

'Good girl, your grandfather just pushed me back into the world after a short yet long walk on that snow!'

Teniola was perplexed. She looked at her mum, wondering if they had actually visited a man on planet Earth. She had visited Pa James before, long ago when she was younger. She knew him as a gentle, loving grandfather who told heart-gripping African moonlight tales. She now could not understand the transformation from a soothing storyteller to a scary one.

'I've always warned your father never to push me out into this world again, but he kept throwing me out,' Pa James continued with a tinge of frustration.

'This is serious,' Teniola thought. 'I have never seen anyone embrace death like Pa James.'

'I have embraced life before death, and what else am I waiting for?' Pa James queried no one in particular.

Teniola hit the roof! 'Was he reading my thoughts?' she asked herself.

Phebean cut in, 'Baba, you are still on planet Earth. You are with humans, so behave like one! And by the way, you are scaring Teniola with your utterances?' She then raised her eyebrows sarcastically and said, 'Please keep your eye open whenever you pray. This will prevent you from seeing my father again!'

Obviously, she had known Pa James to speak in this frightening manner.

As bold as a lion, Pa James continued his narration, 'Your father said that there were more rooms in heaven than in hell. He said hell was not made for humans but rather that hell was purposefully built for Satan and his agents—the demons.'

Pa James continued further, 'As we kept walking and talking, we got to the *Junction of Separation*, and my shadow that had been following me announced the destination and then departed. Your father was on my right-hand side, and we proceeded towards the first junction, which led to another two separate roads. There were descriptions on each side of the road. The road to the left was wide and big, leading to hell, as the signpost read. And I could see millions of people, now dead, moving unobtrusively and uncontrollably towards the road which forked to the left. They could not resist the transiting force pushing them towards this road. It seems that they knew and accepted that the road to the left was destined for them, a "worthy" reward for all they had done on earth. These were souls of those whose names were not written in the Lamb's book of life. They were countless in number—like the seas' sand. They could not be counted. Some were "pastor vultures" in sheep's clothing. I saw many world entertainers flowing freely to hell. I saw worldly millionaires, presidents of nations, rulers of the world, evangelists in the body of Christ, all shuffling freely to hell. I began to shiver. The transition was like five thousand souls at every second of the clock going through the gates of hell. There was a giant creature at the signpost of this road. This living "thing" was the ugliest I've ever seen in my life. I cannot describe it, its description beats my imagination.'

He went on, 'The other side of the road, the right-hand lane, was a very narrow road. The road was very narrow on both sides—and rough too. It could only take one person at a time, no extra room. The road was so compact that souls fitted snugly into it, like a hand in a closely fitted glove. The signpost read: "Welcome to the narrow way, the way that leads to life." There was a huge creature standing at this signpost, a beautiful creature, unlike the horrible creature at the road to hell. The creature on this narrow way was an angel. His height reached to heaven, his right arm opened in a welcoming gesture towards the narrow road. This road was deserted and empty unlike the busy road of hell, where millions of souls shuffled through unconsciously. Sometimes, maybe five souls passed the narrow way in a day. This number was not pleasing to the Lord, who had stood at the far *end junction*. There were about fifteen *judgement junctions* that each soul must pass through before finally making it to heaven. The Lord prepared the narrow way and heaven for man, whom He created in His own image. The devil deceived and misled man into hell. So whenever these few souls whose names were written in the Lamb's book of life shuffled their feet unconsciously through the narrow way, God rejoiced that some had made it through. These souls continue from the narrow way to the next judgement junction.

'On both roads, souls could not control their movement. These movements happened in order, systematically and methodically. No mistake about the chosen path from souls on both ways. All souls were always shaking, looking miserable because they were unsure of their final destination.'

Now, there was complete silence. Teniola listened conscientiously, wanting Pa James to continue his account of the life beyond. Though Teniola was acquainted with what the book of Revelation says about life and death, it seemed that hearing from a man who had just 'been there' pierced through her heart and tasked her soul to search and check all her deeds whilst on earth. She was totally engulfed. The trouble she had bottled up in her mind found nowhere to stay. The burden trailing her from America seemingly disappeared at that moment.

Again, Phebean interrupted Pa James's speech. 'Thank you for letting us know what heaven looks like, we have other issues to discuss with you,' she said. Phebean loved Pa James so much that she habitually protected him from saying things he saw about heaven. The thought of Pa James not returning or not opening his eye again petrified Phebean.

'I wasn't shown heaven yet!' Pa James retorted.

'Teniola is here on a visit from America. She had a challenge with her marriage, please help her in prayer,' Phebean said.

Pa James shifted in his seat to the right and then went still for a moment. At this time, it was difficult to ascertain what was going on in his mind, daydreaming or praying—it was anyone's guess!

'Problem in her marriage?' he momentarily repeated.

'Her husband is . . . ,' Phebean began to pour out, when Pa James again shifted in his seat to the left.

'Let us pray,' he said.

Again in the middle of his prayer, there was complete stillness. Pa James was snoring!

Phebean and Teniola opened their eyes, looking at each other. Phebean shrugged in total surrender to whatever Pa James was doing.

Five minutes later, Pa James eased out of his sleep. 'Jacob of old dug more wells until he reached Rehoboth, his place of rest. Teniola is yet to reach her Rehoboth,' Pa James poured out.

'What does that mean?' Teniola asked.

'Your husband abuses you mentally and constantly beats you up,' he quizzically asked, looking at Teniola for a response. He continued, 'I can see many women flocking around him. You are not on his mind. He once loved you.'

Teniola was now at the edge of her seat. All that Pa James said was true. She had endured both physical and emotional trauma from Rob, her husband. She had prayed and fasted for a turnaround in her marriage.

'You compromised to get married to this man. Strands of his abusive attitude were apparent at the time of your courtship, but you compromised and got married to him,' Pa James alleged.

'You are a believer. Why did you get yoked with the world? Didn't you know that a woman cannot change a man? What you see is what you get! You either wait until he becomes a believer before you date him, or you run completely away from such a relationship.'

Teniola started thinking fast. 'You are very correct, sir. He is not a believer,' she replied slowly. 'I hopefully thought I could change him once we got married. I was lost in love.'

Pa James's sociable voice began to turn gruff. 'That wasn't love, it was lust of the flesh. Teniola, you followed the flesh, you were not brought up that way.'

Sensing that Pa James was getting agitated, Phebean pleaded, 'Okay, Baba, please join us in praying for the husband and for the success of the marriage.'

'All right, if that's what you want, let us pray,' he said.

'Prayer again? We've just finished one, and you were snoring in the middle of it,' Phebean queried.

'Oh yes, that was true. Angels were showing me my mansion at that time,' Pa James responded, gracefully adjusting his attire, a gesture showing his preparedness for heaven. 'Now let us pray again, and I promise not to sleep!'

'How is that possible?' Phebean asked, taunting him.

'It is possible,' said the old veteran as he began to pray. 'You haven't reached your Rehoboth yet,' he repeated after his prayer.

'Baba, I kind of understand what you are saying, but please be explicit. What do you mean by my Rehoboth?' Teniola asked.

'You have to dig another well,' he said. 'Your Boaz is not far off.'

'She will remarry!' Phebean exclaimed.

'God forbid!' Teniola responded in disgust. She snapped her two fingers in their traditional way of saying 'never'.

Pa James smiled. He looked up and stared at Teniola again through his one eye.

'Can you remarry?' He frowned, looking unsure if he had said the right thing.

'No, Baba, and never! This marriage is for better and for worse,' Teniola answered. She was now twitchy and could not bear the thought of getting separated from her husband, not even after all the pain and sufferings she had endured.

'God is not confused, and He will never confuse you,' Pa James enthused. 'He will not violate your right to choose. God will not force this man to stay with you. I see this man divorcing you for another woman, he is leaving—unless he turns to Christ. He once loved you, but it was all lust. Go in peace, it is well with you,' Pa James answered.

'Baba, I know God speaks with you. We still can pray for Rob to stay in this marriage. I don't want my daughter in a second marriage,' Phebean pleaded.

'You have not visited your father's cocoa farm for a while now. You need to check those workers,' Pa James responded, drastically changing the subject matter.

One crucial fact Phebean had learnt during her stay with Pa James was that he didn't believe in preambles. He went straight to the point, and he said things as they were. She knew Pa James had foretold all; he couldn't say any more. There was nothing to add to it. And he could not lie. So at this junction, Phebean accepted fate and decided to go with the flow of his new dialogue. She looked worried though. She wiped a trickle of sweat from her forehead and then replied, 'We'll keep on praying, God is forever on His throne. Meanwhile, let's check on the cocoa farm as you have said.'

Pa James arose smartly from his seat, reaching out for his farm coat. Teniola watched him and marvelled at his agility. A ninety-year-old man still strong, nimble, and mentally alert. She refused to accept Pa James's verdict on her marriage. She rose and stood by the doorway, waiting for her mum and Pa James to finish their tête-à-tête on the cocoa farm.

'I can't leave my husband, I can't leave Rob. God will change him and turn his heart from those strange women,' she consoled herself.

Pa James put on his cap and led them to the cocoa farm. Both Pa James and Phebean laughed and had a nice time remembering old times. Teniola avoided speaking with Pa James on Rob's matter. As they prepared to go back to the city, walking towards their Mercedes Benz, Pa James held Teniola's hands and blessed her. 'I hope to see you soon.'

Teniola giggled with a weak smile, knowing she didn't want to come back to Pa James's house.

'In the next two years, we shall see again?' Pa James threw another bombshell.

'Eemmm . . . I can't tell, Baba,' Teniola stammered.

'All right, go in peace, and greet your husband for me,' concluded Pa.

'Yeah right, my husband indeed,' she mumbled.

She gestured to Seni, her mum's driver, to open the door. Seni opened the passenger backdoor for her and hurried round to the front, sliding in behind the steering wheel. Seni waited for Phebean to bid her final farewell to Pa James after he hurriedly hooped round to the back door and opened it for Phebean too. He adjusted himself behind the wheel, geared up, and slid gracefully away.

ABIOLA AWOLOLA

# CHAPTER 2

# Love Tug of War

IN THEIR ELEGANTLY seated positions at the rear of the vehicle, Tenny warned her mum not to bring her to Pa James's house again.

'He is my uncle, the one I call father. You are obliged to pay him a visit whenever you are in this country,' Phebean responded.

'Teniola, do not let your emotions run over your sense of judgement. You too can pray. God sees all things and He will direct your path. I do not want your countenance so low again. I have watched you since we left for the cocoa farm, you avoided speaking with Pa James.'

'Hey, Mum, don't start the Pa James issue!' Tenny was becoming infuriated. 'Where are we going now?'

Phebean was bothered about Tenny's emotional challenge. 'You have to be more patient in—'

'Mum, where are we going?' Tenny interrupted.

'That was rude. You children nowadays, once you live in the Western world, you tend to behave like them. We don't get rude to parents here in Africa, you hear me?'

There was silence, then a burst of laughter from Tenny. 'My! My! You've always been a funny, sweet mother. Wasn't I born and raised in Nigeria, in Africa? Okay, I'm sorry.' She leaned her head against her mum's shoulder.

'Don't let this Rob guy run you mad. Be who you are and stay focused.'

'Yes, ma'am.' She giggled.

'Well, I want to introduce you to your new tenants. You have not been to your new house since you've arrived. The tenants in this new house are more reliable and peaceful,' Phebean began.

Phebean and her husband helped Teniola in the running of her Nigerian real estate business, a venture she once shared with Rob, her husband, but he seemed uninterested in anything about her. He seemed not bothered about her success or her failure. He was just an individual. He would regularly tell Teniola, 'Do your own and I do mine, I practise individualism.'

'It's a quadraplex house. One of your tenants named Kwame will be leaving soon because of the government's directive to all Ghanaians to return to their country. He is caught in the web.'

'I heard about it too, what a shame. What job does he do?' Teniola asked.

'He is a teacher.'

They reached the new house and alighted from the car. Teniola's smiley facial expression showed it all. She liked the house.

'Thank you, Mum, this is beautiful.' Tenny smiled, showing the dimples nature had beautifully dug into her cheeks.

They heard voices coming from one of the apartments. They moved closer and saw neighbours gathered inside Mr Badmus's living room. They saw Kwame there too.

'Good afternoon, everyone,' Phebean began.

Dozens of eyes zoomed towards their direction. 'Good afternoon, ma'am,' they chorused courteously.

'Thank God you are here,' Mr Badmus began, thereby relieving Phebean and Tenny of the suspense they were kept in. 'Madam, please tell your tenant to leave my daughter alone. He wants to forcefully drag her with him back to Ghana.'

'Why?' Phebean asked.

'Madam,' Kwame quickly interrupted, 'I have been dating Zainab for a while now, and we planned to get married. But as you must have heard, I have to return to Ghana because of the current government directives. I'm here to plead with Zainab's dad to approve our relationship and consent to my marrying his daughter, but he could not just come to terms with our relationship.

'Zainab is an adult, a graduate, and she is working. She knows what she wants. She wants me, and above all, we are both in love. I can and will do anything possible to make sure we remain together. I will take care of Zainab.' Kwame looked in Mr Badmus's direction.

'You see, madam, this is what this Ghanaian man's been singing like the king's market bell for the past one hour. I am Zainab's father, and I insist she stays here with me in Nigeria.'

'Ghana is too far, and besides, we don't know any member of his family,' added Mrs Badmus, who had been sitting quietly beside her husband. 'How can we consent to giving our daughter to a total stranger? A stranger to my family, a stranger in my country!'

Echoes of laughter rent the air. 'It is true, Kwame is a stranger in a foreign land,' teased Kwame's Nigerian friends.

'My people, you are not making it easier on me. You are my people. My mum had visited me here before, and you all saw her here,' Kwame answered, looking mournful, barely able to smile.

As Phebean asked where Zainab actually was, Zainab emerged from one of the rooms, apparently listening to all that was said.

'How are you, Zainab? I'm sure you've been listening to all that Kwame had said and your parent's position on the issue. What do you have to say?' Phebean asked.

'Ma'am, I love Kwame. We have dated for two solid years. It is difficult to throw away this investment called love just because of government directives. Love is stronger than any law or directive. It can stand the test of time. Love is a beautiful thing. It was hard for me to fall in love. I have pleaded with my parents that Ghana is just a few hours by flight from Nigeria. I will send them air tickets to visit us in Ghana.'

'Who said you are going to Ghana?' the mother spontaneously asked. 'Look, Mr Yeboa,' she yelled. 'Your trick will not work here. You see, this daughter of mine is definitely not going with you to Ghana—get that straight to your head. I'm sure you can get a wife when you get to Ghana. What is all this now? Can somebody please help me here!' she asked, turning to the gathered crowd.

'All right!' Phebean interrupted before Kwame could respond to the allegations. 'This issue has two arms. Zainab, I totally agree with your parents. Kwame is a stranger and a sojourner in this country. It will be hard for any parent to willingly give their daughter in marriage to any stranger. On the other hand, you parents have to allow Zainab to follow her heart. She said it was difficult for her to fall in love, and here she is in love with Kwame. The four of you will have to seek further counselling on this.'

Phebean digressed. 'By the way, allow me to introduce to you your real landlady, my daughter, Teniola. She lives in America. We helped her buy this house whilst she was in America.'

'Auntie'—Zainab turned to Teniola—'please help plead with my parents, Kwame is who I love,' Zainab entreated. Her speech caught Teniola unaware.

Teniola, who had been quietly listening to the drama, was gobsmacked. She glanced deeper at Zainab, using the moment to gather words in her brain.

'Well . . . ,' she finally began to speak. 'Have you both prayed on this relationship? Have you sought after God's position in this relationship?' Tenny gathered momentum.

Both Kwame and Zainab were still for a moment. They looked at each other.

'Thank you, madam,' Mr Badmus maliciously interrupted, not giving the two lovebirds time to answer Teniola's question. And truly, he didn't want them to answer the question as he could anticipate their response to be positive.

Regardless, their response found a way through. 'Yes, we know God wants us to be together,' they both replied.

Tenny was now a judge, a judge over a love war—a war in which she had battled for years without success! She began dispensing justice. 'You are now at a crossroad in the relationship. I will advise you to seek God's face further. He is the only one that can lead you aright, no one else—not your parents, not even yourselves—lest you follow your emotions . . .'

Tenny was getting emotional. She was dispensing comfort for herself too. She was strategically mapping her way out of the stubborn siege that held her down. She was gaining relief as she spoke. She didn't want to stop talking; she desired a complete cure for her emotional ailment.

Phebean looked at her watch and was getting impatient. 'We can't stay any longer here. I want to show Teniola around the house,' Phebean cut in, signalling to Tenny to follow her. Tenny was hesitant. She dragged a foot and halted the other.

'Seek His face,' she emphasised.

'God will help resolve your problems.' Phebean turned towards Kwame, and she patted him on the shoulder. 'We will miss you. Pray over it, and God will direct your path.'

The two ladies left the gathering, walking towards the second building.

The discussion continued in Mr Badmus' room. Phebean and Tenny kept themselves busy inspecting the house.

'That was very good advice,' Phebean said after walking away from the Badmuses' apartment.

'Mother, the saying goes, experience is the best teacher. I have learnt my lessons. I have to teach others not to fall into the same ditch I fell into.'

'God will help you out of the ditch, we'll keep praying,' Phebean responded.

They left for home, and Teniola spent another two weeks in Africa before returning to America.

# CHAPTER 3

# Bitter Reality

TENIOLA'S FLIGHT TOUCHED down at the New York International Airport. Leaving the aircraft, Teniola walked down towards the immigration stand and other security checkpoints before finally reaching the arrival hall. It was here that she noticed a familiar face waving at her. It was Bimbo, her closest friend and a business associate. Thousands of questions ran through her mind on why Bimbo was at the arrival hall. She earnestly prayed for her company, Tenny Corporation, the only connection that linked Bimbo to her. She perceived the company as the only reason why Bimbo would come to meet her at the airport.

'Hey, girl . . . nice to see you again,' Bimbo hollered in an American fashion.

'I'm surprised to see you, girlfriend. What are you doing here?' Teniola asked, reaching out to Bimbo for an embrace.

'I knew your so-called Rob would not show up to pick you up, sooo'—she twisted her head—'I made a contingency plan to receive you home.'

Teniola's eyes were already soaked with tears. 'You came for me? Bims, what would I do without you? Thank you.' They both hugged.

'Come on, that's why we are soulmates. Let's move the trolley to the car park.'

Driving home, Teniola was in deep thought, wondering why Rob had not come to pick her up from the airport. And Bimbo, sensing her thoughts, broke the silence that had engulfed the atmosphere. 'Tenny, you've received so much hurt and pain from Rob, you have to decide and make up your mind what next to do. You cannot continue like this. You've kept pouring love into a leaking cup, you will forever be pouring and eventually run out of love soon,' Bimbo cried out.

Teniola burst into tears. 'I don't know how else to please Rob. I love him. I can't get him out of my mind.'

'Listen, girl, this marriage is not working. It's either you blank him completely out of your mind and occupy your mind with other meaningful things, or you lose your mind. You have to think fast. Rob is seen everywhere with different women every day. He has dishonoured you so much by bringing these women into your matrimonial home. How on earth can you still love such a man? What other evidence do you need to prove to you that Rob does not love you any more?'

'Please stop saying that! Rob loves me, and I love him. He will soon realise his mistakes and come back to me. I'm going on another seven days of fasting and praying to save my marriage.'

They were at Teniola's house by this time. The entry gate was left wide open; the house looked deserted. Teniola's heart skipped, beating fast.

'I hope Rob has not brought another woman into the house,' she said in a low voice.

'There is only one way to find out, let us go into the house,' Bimbo answered.

They eased out of the car and slowly walked into the cute and beautiful apartment purchased by Teniola. The house was empty. Rob was not there, and there was a handwritten note on the table addressed to Teniola.

'Look, here is a note for you,' Bimbo said, handing over the note to Tenny.

It read:

*Teniola, I've gone to whom I love, sorry.*

*Rob*

'No, it can't be. Rob cannot write this, someone is playing pranks on me,' Teniola yelled.

'Shut it, Tenny! No one is playing pranks on you. This is Rob's writing, he has gone.' Bimbo held Teniola on both shoulders. 'Please let go of this heartbreaker. He has not offered you anything good except heartache and constant weeping. He has gone.'

Teniola wept. 'I love you, Rob, I love you,' she cried.

'Well, he said he does not love you. Let go of the good-for-nothing man,' Bimbo answered as she made her way back to the car to help offload Teniola's luggage.

On her return, as she laid down the suitcase, she advised, 'As you are now, I can't leave you here on your own. I will pass the night with you. You have to let go of the heartless being.'

Teniola sobbed throughout the night. She called Rob's mobile phone countless times. Early in the morning, she got herself ready to check whether Rob was at his friend's house. Rob, after all never had a job anyway.

'Where are you rushing to this early morning? You've just returned from a long trip. Why don't you rest?' Bimbo asked, having constantly checked on Teniola to ensure she was all right.

'I'm checking for Rob at Clem's house, he might be staying with him.'

'So what if he's staying with Clem? Do you want to force him back home?'

'Bims, please be compassionate, this is my husband we are talking about. Please give him that little honour.'

'Honour indeed! Anyway, I'll come with you.'

They met Clem sitting outside on the balcony of his apartment.

'Morning, Clem, is Rob staying with you?' Teniola asked, eagerly waiting to hear something that would gladden her heart.

'I'm sorry, Lady T, Rob is not,' Clem answered with a pitying eye on Teniola. Lady T was the pet name Rob gave to Teniola earlier in their relationship when the going was good.

'Lady T,' Clem continued, 'you are a beautiful and hard-working woman, yet not appreciated by Rob. Though I'm not in a position to advise you to leave Rob, I am obliged to inform you that Rob had moved in with one of the nightclub girls. I owe this disclosure to you because of your kindness to me. I can't hide such information from you. I want you to move on with your life. Rob doesn't deserve you.'

Clem's exposé was a dagger to Tenny's throat. She thought she had died and came back. She opened her eyes and found Bimbo sitting on the bare floor behind her and Clem with a bowl of water.

'What is all this nonsense?' Bimbo yelled. 'Is your grave here at Clem's house?'

'Hey, woman, or whatever you are called.' Clem's tone became grumpy, turning to Bimbo in response. 'There is no grave here and your friend will not die here.' Clem hurriedly lifted Tenny from the floor. 'You two have to go now.'

Bimbo ignored Clem. Looking back at Tenny, she hissed, 'At what age do you want to kill yourself because of a man? Did I say a man?' Bimbo frowned. 'Sorry, I meant a scumbag. If you continue this way, I will leave you here. Come on, let's go home. Life continues.'

Tenny was pulled into the car, and Clem bade them goodbye.

Bimbo drove back to Teniola's house in silence. Teniola leaned heavily on the headrest, thinking of no one else but Rob, her husband. She thought about the past, the love they both shared during their university days, which gradually disappeared after they got married. She had put her everything into the marriage; she seemingly was repaid with sleepless nights of loneliness and heartache. She had done all that she could; there was nothing left undone. Whilst in these thoughts, suddenly she groaned in her spirit. She wanted to fight her way out of this madness, a way out of the satanic siege that had held her captive for so many years. She had taken pleasure in the love and respect showered on her by all and sundry, but the strength of this pleasure drained each time she set her eyes on Rob. He treated her as someone begging to be loved.

'I don't give love,' he once informed her.

Teniola wanted peace in the midst of this, but she couldn't control her thoughts. She struggled to get rid of Rob's face. She burst into tears again.

'Come on, girl, you have to grow up,' Bimbo began. 'When will you move on?'

'I want to move on, Bimbo, but I cannot help nor control my feelings. I keep thinking about Rob.'

'Try more, babe, you've got to try more. Try and get him out of your mind,' Bimbo consoled.

Teniola looked into the open space as Bimbo drove. When they got home, Bimbo made a cup of tea and served Rich Tea biscuits. Teniola appreciated Bimbo's help and company. She wanted to write; she wanted to console herself. Yeah, she was a very brilliant and successful woman. She had to find a way to encourage herself to fight her way out of depression. She wanted to write a poem, a sonnet she could cherish in case Rob never showed up. She rose, walking toward the bedroom.

'Where are you going?' Bimbo asked.

'I need a pen and paper,' she replied. 'I am going to my room.'

'You want to write to him?' Bimbo asked.

'No, I want to console myself. I want to write a poem.'

'Is this a new style? I've never heard such before—to console yourself through a poem? Okay, I'll get your pen and paper. Where are they?' Bimbo asked.

'Inside my briefcase, upstairs in my room.'

Bimbo brought the briefcase down to Tenny, who wrote:

Dark and lovely I am
Endowed by nature with beauty and virtue
Born like every other woman
But sought after wisdom like no other woman
Wisdom took me to the pinnacles of riches and wealth
But I found love not
While the noble one was at his table
My beauty spread to him like fragrance
A fragrance he could not resist
He humbled himself, laid his glory beside me
He said to me, follow wisdom and not your emotion
Love is here, allow it to grow
But I chose him not; the noble one is not charming enough
He is not handsome, I'd said
Then in the dance house, the charming prince entered
My emotion led, my beloved wisdom eluded me

ABIOLA AWOLOLA

Follow me home, he said to me
All night long in his house
I looked for the one my heart loves
I looked for him but did not find him
He'd left me in the cold hour of the night
Back to the dance house he returned
He danced away with another woman
In my lonely state, I listened to a voice I once ignored
Wisdom whispered, please open the door of your heart to me
You've danced backward; I waited where you once stopped
Pick up your pieces and follow me, wisdom said.

'May I see what you've written?' Bimbo requested, having waited at the dinner table to read Teniola's so-called poem.

She took the sheet of paper from her and read it through. She paused and looked at Teniola in suspense.

'Well done, babe, this is a step to get out. This will encourage other women to pick up their pieces and move on.'

Teniola gave a feeble grin, clinging to the hot cup of tea for warmth.

# CHAPTER 4

# Tears of Wisdom

'NOW LET'S TALK about work, our business, your corporation.' Bimbo changed the topic. She had been longing to tell Teniola of the new business venture. It all happened whilst Teniola was in Nigeria. It was one of the reasons she waited at the airport, not knowing that Rob had moved out.

'You see, girlfriend, I was introduced to some South Korean businessmen, and they are interested in our portfolio. In the last three weeks, I have been conducting feasibility studies on the success of this business should we venture into it. And I can tell you, it is exceptionally viable. Fifteen per cent risk identified, low-risk classification. Eighty-five per cent potential,' Bimbo explained with great excitement.

Teniola smiled, but not blossoming as she would have done if Rob had not moved out. 'What is the nature of the business?' she asked.

'The South Koreans were initially in the process of packaging and delivering some orders to the Nigerian government, but the middleman could not finance the project any more, so he pulled out—and these products are needed by next month,' Bimbo further explained.

'Really?' Teniola asked, showing a little bit of interest.

'Tenny, this is a project we can fund. We have more than enough capital. We are capable of handling this project. Please, let's go for it. We need a round-table meeting to evaluate the SWOT analysis as soon as possible. I don't want us to lose this once-in-a-lifetime opportunity,' Bimbo begged.

'All right, it sounds interesting. And once *you* say a business is viable, I can bet my life on it that it will be a complete success. We'll discuss further in the office tomorrow. Any other activities in the office?' Tenny asked.

'Yes, you need to approve the invoice payment for Radiance Associates. They have delivered the second phase of the project. We are now on milestone two of their payment plan.'

'What percentage is the payment retention on that project?' Tenny asked.

'Tenny, wake up from your slumber! We have a policy of 10 per cent payment retention on all projects, you remember? The nightmare is over, wake up.'

'Oh yeah, that is true, 10 per cent retention. I'm getting round to it, girlfriend, give me more time.' She smiled.

'There are greater things ahead. I've written it clear, let's run with it,' Bimbo encouraged her friend.

They laughed and watched TV. Bimbo suggested Teniola take some herbal stress relief before going to bed to clear her head for the morning. Teniola obliged. They went to sleep.

Teniola slept like a baby, though she remembered Rob when she woke briefly.

Up bright and early in the morning, Bimbo made breakfast for herself and her friend.

'Morning, Bimbo, I want to thank you for everything. You stood by me in the time of my trial and held me when I fell. You took my business like your own, and you see my success as yours. I am eternally grateful to you,' Teniola said.

Bimbo moved closer to Teniola, wrapping her arms around her neck. 'This is why we are friends, to help one another. Your mum called while you were still in bed.'

'Mum from Nigeria? Oh! My God, I have not called her since I returned to America.'

'Yeah, she was worried and asked if you were all right. I told her Rob moved out of the house, and you were disturbed. She wants you to call in the next two hours. She is with your grandpa, Pa James. She asked me to tell you.'

'Pa James, oh my God, he said it, the prophecy . . .'

'What prophecy?' Bimbo asked.

'You see, Bims, I saw Pa James in Nigeria, and he predicted Rob leaving me for another woman. He said that I followed the flesh and got married to him. He even said that I did not seek God's face before marrying Rob.'

'Your grandfather was right, we both followed the flesh. Remember how my relationship with Ade collapsed like a pack of cards! We did not seek His face enough. Anyway, give Mum a call in an hour's time.'

Teniola still struggled with her emotions, but she was determined to brave up, if not for anything but for Bimbo—her pillar of strength. She got herself ready, and Bimbo drove to the office.

Tenny Corporation was formed and owned by Teniola. It served as her breakthrough in the market after several attempts at various business ventures. Her sheer determination paid off, and Tenny Corporation was formed and to date had been very successful. Bimbo, her childhood school friend (whom she later met at a church conference in Long Island City), emerged as an amazing asset, and had since taken Tenny Corporation to greater heights. Bimbo rose to the position of deputy chairperson of Tenny Corporation. Honestly, Teniola dared not make any business decision without Bimbo.

'Should we start the day with a brief conference on the South Korean business?' Bimbo asked.

There was silence; Teniola's mind was miles away.

'Tenny, are you listening? Should we start the day with a quick conference meeting on the South Korean business?' she asked again, this time impatiently.

'Oh, yes. Why not?'

Bimbo knew she was thinking of Rob again. They walked into the office, and Bimbo stopped at Maria's desk. Maria was Tenny's personal assistant; Bimbo needed her to schedule an afternoon meeting with Tenny and the senior management team. She also instructed the accounts payable department to forward all invoices pending approval for payment to Teniola for final signing.

Meanwhile, Teniola was in her office and could not concentrate. Tears flowed uncontrollably; she couldn't help it.

Her phone rang; it was Bimbo. 'Tenny, have you approved the Radiance invoices? This must be done before our afternoon meeting.'

'I'll do just that'.

Two hours had elapsed. Teniola still had not signed the invoices, neither was she ready for the afternoon conference.

She picked up her bag and walked towards Maria.

'Tell the chauffeur to bring my briefcase to the car,' she said whilst walking out of the office.

'But, ma'am, you have a meeting in the next ten minutes, and besides, you have not approved the outstanding invoices,' Maria cried out.

Teniola stopped, paused for a moment, seeming unsure of what to do next. She suddenly proceeded towards the door.

'What do I tell Bimbo?' Maria again asked.

'Tell her I've gone home, I need a break.'

'Home on another break?' Maria echoed to herself. 'But you've just returned from a three-week break!'

'Suit yourself, Maria. I need a break, full stop,' Teniola responded.

Maria was the diehard type. She had the same dedicated spirit as Bimbo, selfless and sacrificial for the success of Tenny Corporation. These three females were inseparable. Though it was very difficult for Maria to accept no for an answer in most cases, Tenny still accommodated her excesses because of her dedication.

Teniola stared into the street as the car moved smoothly. Back at home, she made herself a cup of coffee and sat by the fireplace, getting the warmth she so desperately needed. She couldn't think straight; she just stood staring at nothing. She was taken aback when she heard and saw her front door flung open by Bimbo.

'You left without approving the Radiance invoices. We are in breach of our eight-day payment term. And we are now in breach of our contract. We will incur penalty charges if by tomorrow morning their invoices are not approved! You've also cancelled our meeting for the South Korean business.' Bimbo now moved closer to Teniola, who at this time was surprised at Bimbo's audacious attitude and determination to get the message across to her.

'If the South Korean deal fails, I will quit Tenny Corporation,' she threatened. Teniola knew Bimbo to be determined; Bimbo never played with words.

Bimbo placed a brown paper bag in the middle of the dining table. 'I got you lunch,' she said sharply. 'Let me give you a piece of advice, read your poem again, maybe it will help out, as you are about to wreck the empire you've used all your resources to build! And you know what? Rob will not show up to pick up the pieces for you and neither will I, this is a promise.'

Bimbo whispered, 'Tenny, get your poem, read it, or perhaps write another one. Pick up the pieces and move on. Is this not what your so-called wisdom commanded you to do?'

Bimbo walked out and slammed the door.

Teniola bowed her head thoughtfully.

'Wisdom, poem . . . ,' she repeated. She ran to her study, took a pen, and removed a sheet from the photocopier.

She began to write:

> Yes, the charming prince danced away
> Away from me, the one that loved him
> I have wept; I've wet my bed with tears
> Longing for the charming prince to return to me
> But he returned not
> Then I felt her touch—wisdom, my first counsel
> Wisdom kept waiting where I'd first turned away from her
> She waited for me
> I then embraced and followed wisdom
> My energy returned, energy to forge ahead, never to look back
> But my emotions kicked in again
> It reminded me of the charming prince
> I again lost focus and was confounded
> The foundation of my business empire is now shaking
> The charming prince is not here
> Wisdom is here
> Wisdom speaks again

ABIOLA AWOLOLA

Don't allow your years of hard work to go down the drain
The one you called charming will not be there to pick up the pieces
for you
Rise up, soldier, save your empire
And now, I rose

Teniola read her poem over and over again. She went back to the living room, picked up the lunch pack that Bimbo had made and raced back to the office.

# CHAPTER 5

# Here to Stay

'THAT WAS A short break,' Maria said sarcastically. 'Please get the conference room ready for a fifteen-hundred-hour meeting with the board to discuss the South Korean business. And notify Bimbo and other members of the new scheduled time.'

'Yes, ma'am. You are now talking, back to the very Tenny I once knew,' Maria said.

'Hey . . . don't push your luck too far. I might change my mind,' Teniola said jokingly.

'You are here to stay, ma'am,' Maria retorted.

Teniola smiled and walked into her office, searching through the invoices from her in-tray, and she pulled out the Radiance invoice. She logged on to her system to approve the invoice electronically. She then signed the hard copy and called on Maria to forward it to the appropriate office for processing.

She barged her way through into Bimbo's office. 'You dare not quit on me or on Tenny Corporation.'

Bimbo stood. 'Oh hello, Mrs Rob! So what catapulted you back into the office?'

'You dare not quit on me, neither on Tenny Corporation,' Tenny repeated.

'You can't stop kidding me, girlfriend.' They both hugged. 'I knew you would be sensible. You wrote another poem, huh?' Bimbo asked.

'You are not far from the truth,' Teniola responded. 'The poem slung me back here!'

'You've made the right decision, ditch the whole Rob thing,' Bimbo said.

'Oh yeah, girlfriend! Tenny Corporation cannot go down just because Rod is gone,' Teniola said derisively.

'That's the spirit, girl.'

'Bimbo, what can I do without you?' Teniola asked, still holding Bimbo's hands.

'Nothing!' Bimbo teased. 'The meeting request from Maria just flew, popped up on my computer screen a couple of minutes ago. Thirty minutes to go. Have you had your lunch?'

'Nope. I'll have it now, it's here with me.'

'And have you called your mum?'

'I'll call her later tonight.'

After Teniola ate her lunch, they both headed for the meeting. Teniola and Bimbo sat facing each other at opposite ends of the huge oak wood table. Others sat in a neat arrangement, filling the room.

'What is the business name of our South Korean associate?' Teniola asked.

'Bong Chol Supplies,' Bimbo answered.

'Bimbo, please delegate the following tasks:

1.  Run a check on Bong Chol Supplies for authenticity and quality.
2.  If possible, contact the South Korean government and check whether they've had any business dealings with Bong Chol.
3.  Request for Bong Chol's audited account from the last three years.
4.  Request for Bong Chol's bank statements from the last three years.
5.  Request for a recommendation from a reputable business in South Korea on Bong Chol.
6.  Sample of the products in question from Bong Chol.
7.  Unit price of each product.
8.  Possibility of travelling to South Korea to check production etc.
9.  Product guarantee.
10. Terms and conditions.
11. Memorandum of understanding drafted please.

'I would also like to have different global quotations from other companies in the same line of business,' Tenny requested.

'But this Bong Chol was already accepted by the Nigerian vendor, why should we look for further tenders?' Bimbo asked.

'Bimbo, I want to fulfil all righteousness. I want all this information documented, having followed all due process,' Teniola replied. 'And with our vendor, the Nigerian government, I need the following things:

1. Requisition for the product
2. Purchase order raised
3. Acceptance of sample
4. Any particular mode
5. Payment terms
6. Terms and condition
7. Memorandum of understanding drafted.

'When we receive all the required information, then we'll be able to move forward.'

After the meeting, Teniola stayed at Bimbo's house. They had a memorable time together talking about Teniola's encounter with Pa James and the Nigerian tenants, Kwame and Zainab.

'You have given Kwame and Zainab the best advice.'

'I couldn't have said anything better. It was a learning curve for me too. And lest I forget, I have to call my mum.' Tenny reached out for her cell phone, and after her phone call to the motherland, she joined Bimbo in further discussion on their newfound business.

'Back on Tenny Corporation, don't we need to get a third party involved in our Nigerian-Korean business? We need shippers and representatives in Nigeria.' Tenny asked.

'That is true.' Bimbo nodded thoughtfully.

'Do you have anyone in mind?'

'Yes, Temi Williams is good in this field. He is a successful businessman with various tentacles. He can handle any business.'

'Who is Temi Williams?' Teniola asked.

'He used to be my business associate when I was into buying and selling to Nigeria. He is into importing and exporting.'

'All right, let's get him involved as soon as possible then.'

'I'll call him for a meeting tomorrow. Aren't we forgetting something?' Bimbo asked.

'What?' Teniola asked, looking puzzled.

'Have we sought His face over this business venture? We have not prayed yet. Three days fasting and praying?' Bimbo asked.

'I am frail now, three days will be too much for me. I can cope with a day.'

'All right, we start tomorrow?' Bimbo suggested.

'Affirmative.'

They laughed and went to bed.

The following morning, Temi Williams called at the office to discuss their new business partnership.

Temi agreed to the terms of the business, and they decided that he would cover the shipping and collection of the goods at the Nigerian port. It was expected that both Bimbo and Teniola would have arrived by then to finalise everything at the government house.

A series of meetings were held afterwards, and Bimbo travelled to South Korea for verification as directed by Teniola.

'I want a deposit from the vendor,' Teniola demanded.

'Already there is a promise of 25 per cent working capital payment. The remaining 75 per cent will be paid upon completion. So I'll advise we accept the contract without asking for any deposit. This will prove and show our total commitment to the contract,' Bimbo replied.

'No, we can't do that. It is too risky. We are attempting this business for the first time. Our ability to maximise the 25 per cent with our money is enough to prove our commitment to the government. The deposit is refundable. We cannot bend our rules and policies for anybody,' Teniola argued. 'Please let me know when the 25 per cent will be paid,' she requested.

They proceeded with the business, and the goods were shipped to Nigeria through Temi Williams Freight Services. Temi was in Nigeria a week before their arrival. He cleared the goods from the port and headed towards the final destination in the company of Teniola and Bimbo.

Tenny Corporation made a huge chunk of profit from this business. Teniola and Bimbo's joy knew no bounds. They decided to celebrate at a Hilton Hotel restaurant in Abuja. Temi Williams was invited too.

At the restaurant, after wining and dining, they talked about the success of the business.

'What do you intend to do with this big profit?' Temi asked.

'Reinvest into other businesses,' Bimbo answered.

'What sort of business?'

'Enlarging our present portfolio,' again Bimbo answered.

'Have you thought of acquiring an oil well?' Temi asked.

'Oil well!' Teniola, who had been quiet all along, exclaimed. 'Where and how?'

'Good questions. The "where" is here in Nigeria, and on the "how", I will enlighten you,' Temi replied. 'Over the years, I have researched the best way to invest in oil. I'm not talking about how to invest millions but how I can invest in black gold. From what I found, there are multiple ways to gain exposure to crude oil, but with each option came many drawbacks. The best way to invest in the oil business is to actually produce and sell it. When buying oil wells, you are actually buying the oil production apparatus. You are buying a stream of income as long as you can keep the stream flowing. With future stocks and shares, you are simply buying the opportunity to speculate, hoping the price goes up. When buying an oil well or multiple wells, money can still be made if prices drop, as long as the price is still high enough to offset the expense of the operation. One of my companies, T. Will Production, is now in business and pumping oil. I have not looked back since,' Temi explained.

Temi's short description of generating 'sweatless' wealth caught Tenny's attention. 'What is your diary looking like next Tuesday?' Teniola asked, looking sternly at Temi.

'Anything to increase your millions is worth cancelling other appointments for. What time should we meet?' Temi asked.

'Thirteen hundred hours?'

'Confirmed,' Temi replied.

Looking in Bimbo's direction, Tenny said [as she fondly called her sometimes], 'Bims please email Maria to cancel all afternoon appointments for Tuesday. We are meeting Mr Temi Williams.'

'Done,' Bimbo replied, even though she had not moved an inch from where she sat nor opened her laptop to send any email. Nevertheless, Teniola knew and appreciated Bimbo for her tenacious ability and power to deliver.

'Where do we meet?' Temi asked.

'A business lunch on me at the Restaurant Daniel, 60 East 65th Street, New York.'

'Done deal. When is your flight back to New York?' Temi asked.

'Two days from now. When is yours?' Teniola asked.

'Ermm, I can't remember off the top of my head,' Temi answered, looking away. I've got to catch a flight back to Lagos now. See you next Tuesday.' Temi rose and departed.


'What are your thoughts?' Teniola asked Bimbo, who had been quiet throughout the oil well conversation.

'We are in the best period of our lives. Anything Temi touches turns to gold. Let's go for it.'

'Oil business looks expensive. Do you think we can manage it?'

'How much are we looking at?'

'I forgot to ask him.'

'Okay, then, when we get to that bridge, we will cross it.'

'All right,' they both agreed.

'I need to see my parents before leaving the motherland,' Bimbo said.

'Oh, that reminds me of my parents. The thought of Pa James had been holding me down.'

'He is your grandfather, go and see him.'

'I'm not *gonna* see him. I will only visit my parents,' Teniola replied.

'Suit yourself. Let's book our flights back to Lagos.'

At the Nigerian International Airport, Bimbo and Teniola were busy chatting away when Bimbo felt a touch on her shoulder. It was Temi.

'What are you doing here?' Bimbo asked.

'I'm here doing what you are doing here. Travelling back to America, of course.'

'But you said you were not sure . . . ,' Teniola asked.

'Yes, I wasn't sure of the date then, but now I am sure. Don't you want to complete your oil well acquisition lecture?' Temi asked, smiling.

'Do you always smile?' Teniola asked, having noted Temi's ever smiley face.

'It is food for the heart, it keeps me going. Nothing ever bothers me once I keep smiling,' Temi replied.

'That's the best gift nature could ever give,' Teniola responded.

They boarded their flight, and the trio sat together. Again they discussed the oil well business before Bimbo dozed off. Teniola brought out her pen; she wanted to write another poem since sleep had evaded her eyes.

'Are you not sleeping?' Temi asked.

'I will catch a nap soon, but first I want to write a poem.'

'You write poems?' Temi asked.

'Yes, when opportune, I find myself writing poems.'

'Really, I write too, but songs for now.'

'I write songs too. In fact, I have some on my laptop right here.'

'Okay, let me see,' Temi requested.

Teniola opened her laptop and shared one of her compositions:

**Verse one**
God created man in His image
To worship and praise His great works
To serve the Lord with gladness of heart
And to come before Him with singing

**Chorus**
I was born to be a worshipper
To serve the Lord for the rest of my days

ABIOLA AWOLOLA

**Verse two**

When I worship, heaven opens
For God had waited to hear me worship
Angels joined in this treasured moment
And the twenty-four elders, they joined in worship

**Verse three**

When I worship
Know that God is Lord overall
He rules over where men say He cannot
Man has no choice but to worship the Lord
For man cannot live without worship

'Whoa! What a song, what amazing lyrics!' Temi exclaimed. 'These are powerful words. Great work, well done. I can't show you mine as they are not as powerful as yours. The next time we meet, I pray to be bold like you. I'm happy to see that you are a believer like me.'

'I am a born-again Christian,' Teniola responded.

'I'm an elder in my church.'

They continued chatting till they both nodded off, sleeping as the flight gently touched down.

# CHAPTER 6

# Distractions

BACK IN AMERICA, a special delivery was delivered to Teniola's office. She opened it and saw divorce documents from Rob's lawyer. Wobbling with a combination of emotion and despair, Teniola's legs gave way. She sank into her chair, completely void of reason.

'Rob wants a divorce?' she echoed to herself.

She grabbed her phone and made a call straight to Bimbo.

'I need you in my office right away,' she commanded.

Bimbo rushed into Teniola's office only to find her in tears.

'What's the matter?' she asked. 'Is everybody all right at home?'

Teniola handed the letter to her. Bimbo read.

'Is this why you are distressed? Are we taking steps backward after achieving so much without this Rob issue? Tenny, this is another distraction from the devil. Remember, when we were about to hit this jackpot from the South Korean business, the hurdles we had to go through before you could regain your sanity. Come on, girl, the oil well is round the corner, and distraction shows its ugly head again! What should you do?'

There was silence.

'Cut the ugly head off, girl,' Bimbo answered her own question.

Teniola said nothing.

'Tenny babe, sign the divorce letter and send it back to him. Rob is bitter to your tongue. Spit him out of your life once and for all,' Bimbo urged.

'He is still my husband, Bimbo, please don't talk of him like that,' Teniola pleaded.

'Husband indeed! Okay, leave the letter aside for now. At least you have some cooling-off time before responding. Look, I can't risk this oil business for anything. Let's go for a walk then,' Bimbo suggested.

They strolled, returning to the office after thirty minutes of chatting.

'What happens to your poems? They seem to be the only boost that energises you to regain your freedom from Rob's mental bondage.'

'I haven't looked at them for a while now,' Teniola replied.

'You need Rob out of your mind. Now that he is trying to force his weight on to your thoughts, get the poems out! There is a big catch on the way, and we cannot afford to miss it,' Bimbo urged. 'And besides, we are meeting Temi tomorrow for the oil well meeting. You have to be in a very good state of mind before committing to such business.'

'I'm not writing a poem this time, I am singing.' Teniola sang:

And now let the weak say I am strong
Let the poor say I am rich
Because of what the Lord had done
For me
I give thanks.

Teniola went on her knees, right there in her empire, and prayed. She prayed intensely. 'Take this cross away from me, Lord,' she said. 'Give me peace, Lord. Give me rest on every side. I regain my dominance over situations. *I won't be dominated by them!* I regain my freedom, and I am free. Amen, in Jesus' name.'

'Amen. Bravo,' Bimbo responded. 'We are getting on top of things now.'

'Thanks, Bimbo,' Teniola responded.

'She is now charged, back to the vibrant Teniola of Tenny Corporation.'

'As per our meetings tomorrow,' Teniola began, 'please conduct a detailed investigation on the oil well business in all parts of the world. I want the country's name, their prices, their sizes, risks involved, etc. Then beam your searchlight on Nigerian oil wells. If possible, get details of the main players in the business in Nigeria, and we'll prepare some questionnaires for them to help us.'

'Your last request is a bit thorny. Oil well owners in Nigeria may not be willing to share their information with us,' Bimbo answered.

'What we need is just information on how they've survived in the business and how they started. If they can't complete the questionnaire, then we can ask the Americans or the Saudis. I know they will be able to share such. But it will be a thing of shame if my fellow Nigerians cannot contribute to my success,' Teniola said.

'Stop kidding yourself. You know who we are, unless a change comes,' Bimbo replied.

The following day, at the hour stated, Teniola and Bimbo met with Temi at the restaurant. After dining, Temi explained in great detail what the oil well business entailed. Both ladies asked question upon question, just to make sure they were entering the right business. They wanted to fully understand it.

'I will suggest you go for a sandwich course in oil and gas operations to enhance your understanding of the business,' Temi suggested.

'That is the right word,' Bimbo responded. 'I will continue with our research and feasibility studies. Maybe Teniola should enrol for the course.'

'All well by me,' Teniola responded.

The two ladies were preparing to leave when Temi reminded Teniola of his song.

'I've written a new song. Would you like to read it before you leave?' he asked.

'Oh yes. Why not? I love songs.'

'Well guys, I've got to go,' said Bimbo. 'I am not a music person.' She packed her bag and left before Teniola could say anything.

'Okay, let me see what you've got,' Teniola requested.

Temi brought out a folder containing several songs.

'Are these all songs?' Teniola asked.

'Yes, they are,' he responded whilst bringing out a single sheet of paper with a song scribbled on it. 'I'm sorry. I normally type my songs, but I was in a rush this morning.'

'That's fine. Let me have a look please.'

Temi handed over the sheet.

It read:

The fear of the Lord is the beginning of wisdom

Embrace wisdom now

For wisdom cries *at the city gates*

For I'm much precious than silver

Much precious than gold

Much precious than rubies

Embrace me

Jehovah possessed me at the beginning of His ways

Before His works of old, God had me

When God created the heavens, I was there

When he created the universe, I was there

When He formed all humans, I was there

When He packaged your destiny, I was there.

Teniola was soaked in the lyrics of the song, which touched her heart in a manner that made her feel lighter.

'He wrote on wisdom,' she thought to herself.

'Why on wisdom?' she asked, still very sober.

'The Lord asked me to write on wisdom. I had typed a different song on the very day we returned from Nigeria. That was the song I intended giving you until this morning when I heard 'wisdom'. I opened my Bible to the book of Proverbs and checked what pertained to wisdom, then I prayed, but my heart still pressed on wisdom. So I scribed something to meditate upon on my return. On getting here, I heard a voice say, "Give her the song."'

'The Lord asked you to write on wisdom?' Teniola asked. 'My two poems were on wisdom too.'

'It can only get better with Jesus,' Temi replied.

'All right, I've got to go now,' Teniola answered and moved her stuff. They both walked to the main street where they took different taxis to their destinations.

Teniola was stepping out of her car in the parking lot when she saw Rob walking towards her. Her heart sank. She hadn't seen him in over a year, and she hadn't signed the divorce papers.

'Why haven't you signed the divorce papers?' Rob asked.

'Because . . . becau—' Teniola stuttered.

'Because of what, Teniola? You have no reason to delay the divorce process.' Rob was irritated.

'But I still love you, Rob. I have always been there for you.'

'Can't you get it, Tenny?' Rob interrupted. 'I don't love you any more. I was there for you when I could be. I housed you when you finished university and you had nowhere to stay. I contributed towards the purchase of your first car. I even taught you how to drive. Look, Tenny, I hate recounting all I have done for you. And I did appreciate your patience and loyalty to our marriage. The point is that my heart is with somebody else. Furthermore, we are worlds apart. I could hardly secure a job since we both finished uni. Look at you, look at your corporation—known all over America. Where am I in all this?'

'But, Rob, you are one of the directors of this corporation. You refused to step a foot into the corporation. You just aren't interested in anything that is mine.'

'How could I be? Even the house we both lived in was bought by you.'

'But it is registered in both our names. Rob, your name is included in the documentation of this house. My insurance policy is in *your* favour. You are my next of kin in everything. How else do I please you?' Teniola asked.

'It's not about pleasing me, Tenny. I am just not happy in this marriage.'

'We can make it work, let's go for counselling.'

'I'm sorry, Tenny. I want a divorce.'

'It's the club girl, yeah?' Teniola asked.

'Yes, she wants to know when the divorce will come through. I want to marry her.'

'What? You want to marry a club girl!'

'Yes, she is my choice.'

'You chose a club girl over me? Well, I cannot give you a divorce, do your worst!' Teniola responded militantly.

'I will make life miserable for you, Tenny. I advise you to sign those papers and forward them to my lawyer as soon as possible.' Rob walked away.

'You've done worse. I don't expect anything less,' Teniola yelled. She was agitated and felt insulted that Rob could leave her for an ordinary club girl.

'All right, the battle line is now drawn,' Rob shouted back.

Teniola was shaking. She was sad. Rob's words hit her like a sledgehammer. After all her commitment and loyalty to their marriage, Rob preferred a club girl to her. She gathered her strength and walked into her office, determined to make it difficult for Rob to get the divorce.

'What is wrong with you, Tenny? Sign the documents and let go of Rob,' Bimbo bawled. 'You need your sanity and peace of mind. Let go of him. On what grounds is this divorce requested?'

'Irreconcilable differences. The court will decree the marriage dissolved after two years of legal and/or physical separation,' Teniola explained.

'How many months have you been separated from him now?' Bimbo asked.

'Seventeen months now,' Teniola replied.

'You are nearly there. I don't know why you want to hold on when the court will forcefully separate you anyway.'

'I'll wait for the court to separate us. I want God to see that I did everything in my power to save the marriage.'

'Yeah, right,' Bimbo responded. 'Anyway, how far you gone with the oil and gas course? You should have finished by now.'

'I'm finishing by next week. It's quite an interesting course though, and I can tell you, this deal will be the biggest success hit for Tenny Corporation. I am so sure of this, as sure as a mouse can tell cheese from butter.' Tenny's beautiful face glowed with excitement. She envisioned a bigger picture of her oil business.

Bimbo sank into the high-back chair, reaching out for some of the biscuits piled on the plate to her left.

'The oil business is really getting into you, huh? Where is Temi in the picture? When are we seeing him?'

'There is no appointment fixed yet. But first, let me see your oil research report, then we'll arrange to see Temi. Meanwhile, the guy's been looking for a doable oil well in Nigeria. He seems to be more convinced on this business than anything else.'

Bimbo spun around on her chair to face her. 'When it comes to wise business decisions, Temi is the man.'

'You can say that again, girlfriend. It seems he's got that hand of gold.'

'I'm putting the final touches in place before close of play tomorrow.' Rising to her feet, Bimbo continued, 'Are there any other issues apart from your divorce papers and the oil business?'

'The divorce papers!' Tenny groaned. 'You've just reminded me of my estranged husband!'

'Hmmm . . . mmm, like I have said, the oil business has done a great job on your mechanism for you to easily forget the almighty Rob! Well, I've got to leave, if there is nothing else to discuss. I'll see you in the morning.' Bimbo walked out of the office.

# CHAPTER 7

# Options

A S THE WEEK passed by, Teniola carried on as normal and deliberately avoided thinking about Rob. She had developed thick skin, which shielded her from worries and thoughts of Rob. Rob's decision to marry a club girl had ultimately blown everything apart, and as the saying goes, it had broken the camel's back.

'A right-thinking man would not abandon a caring, successful woman for a club dancer, a club girl! Something must be definitely wrong with this Rob of a guy. And I will make the divorce difficult for him. After all, I have nothing else to lose except him!'

She paused. 'Easy exit is not an option for you, Rob. If this is the only pound of flesh I can get back.' She paused again for emphasis. 'A pound of flesh for all the heartache you caused me, then so be it.'

Tenny was finally finding peace in herself and in her separation from Rob. 'Life continues,' she said, and she left for the day.

The following morning in her office, after going through Bimbo's research, Teniola instructed Maria to book Temi in her diary for a meeting.

Tenny reached into her desk drawers and extracted a large brown envelope. She opened it and brought out the contents, some documents—a memorandum of understanding (MOU) to be signed by her and Bimbo. This was a contractual agreement drafted by Tenny to run the oil business together with Bimbo. The contract also detailed the percentage share of ownership in the business. Tenny was to be the main funder of the project under her umbrella company, Tenny Corporation. Bimbo had no financial stake. But Tenny was a giver, a crazy giver. She appreciated all Bimbo's selfless sacrifices for her company and to her personal life. And the only way to compensate more to what she had already given was to give Bimbo a 30 per cent share of the oil business. She tossed the papers on the table.

Bimbo took the papers and began to read. 'This is a contract,' a statement she made.

Tenny nodded slowly. 'Yes.'

'Thirty per cent share?' She paused. 'For me?' Bimbo recoiled on her seat. Of course she knew Tenny was a giver, but 30 per cent share of a multimillion-dollar project was just too mind-blowing.

'You're kidding me, Teniola Davies,' Bimbo dragged the words.

'I ain't kidding you, babe, this is for real.'

'For real?' Bimbo could not conceal her joy any more. She leaped off her seat and landed on Tenny's long legs, her arms wrapped tightly around her neck. It wasn't a warm embrace at all.

'You are choking me,' Tenny groaned in a strangled shout.

'Sorry, babe, I didn't mean to hurt you.'

'Then get your *butt* off my leg!' Tenny pushed Bimbo's weighty flesh to the floor. 'Heavens!' Tenny cried out. 'You had a nice Christmas break, huh? How many chicken drumsticks went into that belly of yours?'

Bimbo was totally disinterested in the last Christmas break or in the number of chicken drumsticks that landed in her belly; she was engrossed in what destiny was opening up for her. She picked herself from the floor, dusted her butt, and began, 'I knew I was destined for greatness immediately after I set my eyes on you in that Long Island City Church Convention.'

'We are both destined for greatness,' Tenny replied, stretching her flexible legs as if her bones were crushed into pieces by a metal substance.

'I'm now a millionaire! I am a millionaire,' Bimbo yelled.

'Hey, wait till we've made some money out of the business before counting your eggs.'

Bimbo laughed. 'Let me tell you something, babe. Digging Mother Earth for oil is one of the most lucrative businesses in the whole world. It cannot fail unless the well dries up or a natural disaster happens.'

'Hmm . . . hmm.' Tenny nodded thoughtfully.

'Oooohh . . . ,' Bimbo roared with excitement. 'You can't understand what I'm saying. This is a wheel of fortune beckoning to me. And knowing that Temi, the business tycoon, is manoeuvring this wheel, it is making me feel like paradise on earth.'

'Now that you've mentioned Temi, we need to get these papers signed before he arrives. Enough of your praises on the 30 per cent share, let's get work done,' Tenny reacted.

She pulled a pen from her chest drawer, took the papers from Bimbo, and signed the two copies of the contract. She tossed them back to Bimbo to sign. She quickly obliged. Tenny took a copy and asked Bimbo to keep the other copy for herself.

'Let's give Him praise.' Both ladies went on their knees and thanked God for the success of their new business venture.


A meeting was scheduled with Temi for the following day.

Teniola arrived late to the office, having been held up in another meeting, so Temi waited for her in Bimbo's office.

Upon arrival, Teniola summoned Maria to call Temi and Bimbo immediately into the conference room. Maria, however, explained that there were other two prior appointments before Temi and that these visitors were waiting.

'Temi is a bona fide partner of this company, please call him in now,' Teniola responded.

'But, ma'am, the other two have waited for over an hour now and—'

'Maria, if Temi leaves these premises without seeing me, you are to immediately tender your resignation letter to me.'

'Resignation . . . what!'

'It is important for you to obey my orders. This is what you are here to do. Tell the other visitors to wait, or you reschedule alternative appointments for them.'

Maria became a moonwalker as she slid out of Tenny's office. She would not risk losing her job for anything in the world—not because she would not find a better job in America, but because she believed she would not find a boss as loyal, kind, and easygoing as Tenny. Maria had developed an informal relationship with her. She even affectionately referred to her as Lady T because of this close yet careful fondness.

Her movement towards Bimbo's office gathered additional impetus. 'Temi,' she mumbled softly, 'you dare not leave without seeing Lady T, and you must wait in that room.' Temi and Bimbo gathered in the conference room. Temi shared in-depth detail with the ladies, clearly outlining the process for acquiring oil wells in Nigeria.

'The first rule for purchasing an oil well is for us to provide the LOI (letter of intent), which will be directed to the seller at the address specified. Once the LOI had been found to be satisfactory by the seller, the seller then returns it to us along with an offer letter. We will also be given the documents of the block so that we can verify them for authenticity. Once we feel completely satisfied with the process, we will then meet one on one with the seller to sign the sales agreement. Once an agreement is signed, the money is transacted, and the transfer of ownership takes place,' Temi explained.

'Can they be easily trusted?' Bimbo asked.

'There are ways to check the authenticity of oil blocks,' Temi explained. 'This is a business I am doing, and I have never recorded a loss. There are currently four contacts sourced for you. I will run through them with you.'

'Whoa! Four contacts already?' Teniola exclaimed.

After rigorous discussions, the trio agreed to send the LOI by the following week and also agreed to travel to Nigeria in the upcoming months. Meanwhile, Temi was busy preparing all that was required for the success of the business. He took it as his own, even though he had no stake in this business. Tenny on her part had prepared to recompense Temi for his trouble after the successful implementation of the oil block. She was not one to take favours for granted. In fact, Tenny was widely known for her generous heart and for giving freely. She was a 'mad' giver. She never defaulted with her tithes (a tenth of her income). She would regularly prepare her tithe before the Lord on bended knees before leaving for church. Tenny first began with the traditional 10 per cent tithes and then increased her giving to 20 per cent. She currently paid 40 per cent, and she never lacked in terms of finance. She'd always say, 'I can't outgive God. A tither spends from the pocket of Jehovah.'

Three weeks after the oil meeting, Teniola was walking into her office when Maria suddenly ran towards her, worried stiff.

'Mr Williams is here to see you. He's been in the premises since 7 a.m. this morning,' Maria explained, looking totally frightened.

'All right . . .' Tenny stuttered, appearing furtive. 'He is here?' she repeated Maria's words. 'Why so early?'

'He said he wanted to see you.'

'So why didn't you call me on my phone?'

'He instructed me not to call you. He preferred to wait until you arrived in the office.'

Fear clutched Teniola's stomach. 'Why? What could have happened? Where is he?' Teniola's roller coaster of questions kept coming. 'In the conference room?'

Teniola raced towards the conference room. Maria raced after her. There she found him sitting up straight and watchfully guarding and trailing the movements of the entrance door. He rose immediately when he set his eyes on them.

Realising their panicked states, he first spoke, 'I'm sorry to have caused this troubled moment. I needed to speak with you urgently.' His smiley face wasn't there any more.

'Are you . . . are you all right?' Tenny stammered.

'Are you all right?' Maria interrupted his response with another question. Tenny eyed Maria before looking back at Temi.

'I . . . I am all right, thank you both,' he responded. 'I just needed to speak with Tenny—alone please.'

'How is the oil business doing?'

'Going accordingly,' he replied with a reassuring smile.

'Should we go into my office then, or you prefer to have the discussion here?'

'Your office please,' he'd said.

'Please come with me.' Teniola shrugged and briskly walked out of the conference room. Maria followed.

'Maria,' Tenny called, 'you may return to your office please.'

Maria wasn't pleased with such an arrangement. She wanted to know what threw the mighty man out of his bed so early in the morning.

In Tenny's office, instead of her usual meeting table, she gestured to the office couch for him to sit on. Temi was hesitant for a while. He, however, strolled to the couch and sat. Tenny sat at the end of the couch, tense in the suspense of what was to come.

'Teniola,' he began slowly, choosing his words carefully, 'what I'm about to say might sound strange to you, but I have to tell you.'

Tenny looked nonplussed. 'Please tell me,' she begged. Her heart was beating faster now.

Temi paused. He looked intently at her and began, 'Teniola, God said you are my wife!'

Teniola's jaw literally hit the floor. Her brain felt fuzzy, airy, and blown away. She shot out of the couch, distancing herself from Temi. She looked at him thoughtfully, unable to find the correct words to use.

'God said what? Which God?' Tenny almost flinched. 'I mean, how could God say that to you?'

'He did.' Temi was affirmative. 'He confirmed this to me in so many ways, even before I met you. He gave me your description and how destiny would bring us together.'

'What did you say, Mr Williams?' Tenny asked, less loudly now. She wondered if Temi had taken a few puffs of ganja before coming to see her. For a second she lost her voice; words became too heavy to utter.

She had considered Temi as a married man with children. 'Are you not married?'

'I am divorced with two children.'

'You're divorced?' she repeated. 'Well . . .' She dragged the word out. 'God hasn't spoken to me about you! And I don't think I am your *so-called* wife!' She spoke with all frankness.

Temi was unruffled by her reaction. He nevertheless continued, 'Please allow me to explain further. These are His exact words: "She is the bone of your bone, the flesh of your flesh."'

Tenny froze. 'Hey . . . Temi, please stop and stop now! You need a break. Please go on holiday and have a *very* long rest. I am not that bone of your bone, neither that flesh of your flesh.'

Tenny's response pierced through his skin; it disorientated him. But knowing what he heard from God, Temi—forty-five years old, bold, intelligent, tall, and brightly handsome—absorbed the rude shock and maintained his tranquil posture. He sat silent, his head bowed.

Tenny seized that opportunity to think about Rob and her marriage. 'Have you ever considered my marital status?'

'God would not call you my wife if you are married. Or are you married?' Temi gave a taunting smile.

Teniola found his smile offensive, but she concealed her annoyance. 'I am not in a position to answer that question of yours. And besides, we are business associates, and it will remain that way. What you have discussed this morning will never exist, and I will take it as a mistake, never to repeat itself again. Do you have any update on our oil business?'

'The oil business plan is going on well. There is nothing to worry about.'

'So then, please take your leave.' Now pointing to the pile of documents on her table, she said, 'As you can see, I have just gotten into the office, and I have a lot lined up for the day.'

Temi rose from the couch and strolled with ease to the door. He stopped and looked back at Tenny who could not take her eyes off him.

'Please pray over this matter. I'm sure I heard Him speak.'

'This conversation never happened.' She looked away, turning her back to him.

He reached for the door and left. She heard the door shut and knew he had left. She sunk into her chair and spun around in disbelief. Was that a trance, a sleep, a dream, a spell—call it whatever!

She summoned Maria to her office right away.

'I don't want to see Temi Williams in this office again unless there is a scheduled appointment,' Teniola instructed.

'But you said he was a *bona fide* partner of this—'

'For heaven's sake! Now listen, thespian, I am in my right state of mind. I am not mad!' Tenny shouted in a sudden fit of anger. 'Yes, I once said he was a bona fide member of this company, but now, I've changed my mind. Can't you get it for once, Maria?' Tenny was upset. She was angry. Maria, unfortunately, was the nearest person to get the heat from her furnace of anger.

Meanwhile, Maria was thinking swiftly. Tenny's reaction puzzled her. 'What could have transpired between this Temi of a man and Teniola?'

'Maria.'

She heard her name called. She jerked out of her thoughts and looked at Tenny.

'I don't want to see him—I mean Temi—without a scheduled appointment, do you get that?'

'Yes . . . yes, ma'am,' Maria stuttered.

Then there was silence. The usually blissful atmosphere of Teniola's office seemed to absorb and retain quietness, blanketing Tenny's bubbling and happy face.

'You may go,' Tenny intoned.

Maria nodded and proceeded to leave.

'Please get in touch with AITT Incorporations. They will be our business consultants for the oil business. And they'll liaise with Temi on my behalf,' Teniola added.

'Yes, ma'am.'

'Lady T is weird. This is a lady that threatened me with the sack if Temi left without seeing her, and now she has banned this same Temi from coming to the office. I have said it before, power is good. I know I will become like Teniola Davies someday. I know I possess those virtues,' Maria mumbled to herself.


Teniola was disturbed. She needed to talk to someone; she wanted to pour her heart out to someone. She put a call to her agony aunt, Bimbo—her loyal friend.

'May I see you in my office now please?' she ordered. The tone of her voice was tenacious. Her every word was filled with urgency.

In no time, Bimbo was there. She knew that such a tone came when serious matters on the corporation were to be discussed. In Tenny's office, she quickly grabbed her usual seat, positioning herself for corporate talk. Tenny was pacing up and down. Bimbo looked up at her, tasking herself ready for a solution to whatever was melting Tenny's heart.

Before she could ask what the problem was, Tenny snarled, 'Temi was here today. He came very early in the morning . . .'

Bimbo's heart skipped. She thought of the oil business, her 30 per cent ownership share and Tenny's 70 per cent. She shifted her buttocks to the edge of the seat. 'Yeah . . . So what happened?'

'What happened?' Tenny reiterated. 'I thought you were in the loop . . .'

'In the loop of what?' Bimbo hurriedly asked.

Tenny was now hesitant. 'Well . . . he came to tell me I'm his wife!'

Bimbo's mouth was ajar; she was unable to get it closed. 'His what? His wife, did you say?'

Tenny now recounted what happened between her and Temi.

'And I turned him away,' Tenny arrogantly ended her narration.

'You turned him away? Just like that? *Haba!* You shouldn't have turned him away.'

'Why shouldn't I?'

'Tenny,' Bimbo yelled. 'What is wrong with you? How long will you continue holding on to your past? Is it a crime for a man to be attracted to you?'

'Bimbo! What are you saying? Is this a plot?'

'I think you should break into a big dance if I should ever have the time in the world to plot this for you. I have a life, girl, go get one!' she yelled. 'And besides, aren't you a woman? Someday you will have to remarry and settle down. Or do you think I will be around, forever wiping your tears from Rob's heartless trauma? Of course not, I am moving on, just like you are supposed to be moving on.'

'Enough of your sermon!' Tenny cut in. 'I would like to be alone please.'

'Suit yourself,' Bimbo replied and strolled out of the office, leaving the door flung open.

# CHAPTER 8

# Tension

TENNY WENT TO the door and shut it; she leaned her back firmly against it. She began to meditate. 'I believe my marriage to Rob is over, but that is not a leeway for another relationship,' Teniola mumbled to herself. 'The divorce papers are still pending signature. Another relationship? No way. I am still married to Rob Ajibade, for crying out loud! I must forget this Temi stuff, he's a dreamer.'

And truly, she was able to blank Temi completely out of her mind—until exactly three days later, when she had a dream.

In her dream, Teniola had a broken stool, and she took the pieces to Temi for repair.

Temi helped repair the stool, and she was happy. She began to dance. She woke up.

She could interpret this dream, but she was determined not to give it a look in. 'There is no chance for Temi,' she said.

She kept the dream to herself; she said nothing to Bimbo. And Bimbo deliberately avoided talking about Temi. Both ladies conversed on business matters only.

The following week, she had another dream.

In Teniola's second dream, she found herself sitting on the stool repaired by Temi. She was in a house she thought to be her own. She was offloading various fruits from her shopping bag when she saw Temi in that same house. He was carrying a basket full of various assorted fruits too.

'What are you doing in here?' she queried.

'This is my house, our house,' Temi intoned.

'Your house, our house?' Tenny reiterated.

'Yes, our house, and you are sitting on the stool I repaired for you.'

They both laughed.

Teniola woke up.

She was not confused. Again, she could interpret this dream. She knew what it meant. She kept it to herself. She was scared, scared of getting hurt from any other relationship. She couldn't trust any man. 'They are unfaithful,' she said.

She had not seen Temi since that last time he dropped the bombshell in her office. He had not called on her since then either.

She got prepared, ready for another exciting day. At the office, she was in the middle of a telephone conversation when she heard Maria's voice. She was arguing with a visitor. Maria's voice was by far the louder in this strange communication. In fact, Teniola noted that she could not hear any response to Maria's loud blast of 'You have to book an appointment'.

'I only need to see her for five minutes,' the visitor said.

'A whole five minutes!'

'You are making it sound like five hundred minutes.'

'That is exactly what it is.'

'What!' Temi couldn't hide his surprise.

'You can hear me well, sir.'

'Oh no, Maria, you can't do this. Please let her know I'm here.'

'So the world should be at a standstill just because you are here?'

Temi laughed. 'You are very funny, Maria.'

'There ain't anything funny, sir. You need to book an appointment, period.'

'Okay. It seems your modus operandi has changed. Is there any slot for today?'

'Nope!'

'Tomorrow?'

'Nope!'

'A day after tomorrow?'

'Nope!'

Temi laughed again. 'This is getting funnier.'

'Tenny's diary is filled to the end of the year!'

Temi burst out laughing. Maria watched in disdain.

'She instructed you to do this, huh?'

'I'm only doing my job, sir.'

'Okay, thanks for being unhelpful.' And he stormed out of the office.

Tenny listened attentively. She maintained her stance. She didn't intervene, and eventually, the noise died down. A few minutes after, Maria raced into her office recounting how she resisted Temi from coming into her office. Tenny gave a disarming smile, her dimples showing the endowment of nature.

'Well done, Maria. For the first time, you are taking to instructions. I don't want to see him here unscheduled,' she restated.

'Yes, ma'am,' Maria answered. 'And may I ask a question please?'

'I know what your question is, and the answer is, it's a private matter. You will get to know in the near future.'

'*Shush me!*' Again Maria mumbled to herself.

'Aye?' Tenny saw her mouth movement but could not hear what Maria said.

'Nothing.'

'Please shut the door after you.'


Teniola finished for the day and was at the car park when she heard a voice, a very familiar voice calling her name. The masculine voice Maria once shouted down over three hours ago—Temi Williams's voice. She stood still, the chilling cold hitting her. She gathered the energy to look back. She hoped the voice would not match Temi's, but unfortunately for her conscience, the manly voice was Temi's. He had waited three hours in his car outside Teniola's office. Her conscience became guilty.

'I have waited to see you.' Each word slipped his frozen lips.

Tenny looked down at her watch. 'Three hours ago,' she stammered.

Teniola shivered. Her legs became weak. The weather was bitterly cold, about minus five degrees Celsius. She could feel the bitter cold penetrating through her thick fur coat within her two-minute stay in the car park. She imagined how the wintery snow would have dealt with him. She moved towards her car and leaned her back against it for support. Shock and surprise were an understatement for Teniola's reaction.

'It is obvious you don't want to see me. What can you make of these words? A broken stool repaired by me, various fruits in my house, our house,' Temi managed to ask, his lips dried up by the frenzied cold breeze.

'Christ . . . Christ . . .' Teniola dragged her words. Her eyelids weighed down with tears. She held on to the car door handle, gripping it tightly for the support of her life, but the ground was failing her. She was slipping away.

'Christ . . . oh! Christ,' she stammered again.

Temi now moved closer to support her, preventing her from losing her balance to the cold floor. Tenny felt the stiff fingers, beaten by the angry snow. She couldn't forgive herself for being responsible for such punishment to Temi.

'Please, Teniola,' Temi began, 'open up your heart and allow God to confirm these words to you.' Temi aligned himself to the car. 'I serve a true and a faithful God. I wouldn't have persisted if He hadn't asked me to come. With the little you've known of me, I am a man of integrity and honour. I wouldn't sit here in the snow waiting to see you if I am not convinced He had sent me. You are a sister and a friend. I would not do anything to hurt you. Please pray over these words.'

Silence enveloped the bitterly cold air; the car park was in complete stillness. Tenny was still lost for words.

'I will give you enough time to think over them,' Temi echoed in pain. The cold had ambushed him, throbbing in his bones and weakening the nerves in his legs. It was his turn to fight the law of gravity, unconsciously falling away.

Teniola quickly held him. Without thinking, she held him tightly in her arms.

'I . . . I . . . saw the stool, the fruits, and the house . . . ,' she answered with sorrowful eyes. 'I saw them. I am sorry. I don't know what came over me.' She bit her lips, and looking into his eyes, she sobbed. 'I had the dream twice, and I knew what they meant.' She wiped her tears with the back of her hand.

'Thank you, Lord.' Temi gathered strength. He pulled himself to stand without her support. He tried to smile, but the smile was swallowed up by his dry, tight face. He lifted his hands to heaven, giving thanks.

'Did God show these to you?'

Temi shrugged. 'Yes, He instructed me in my dream to mention them to you.'

'Oh heaven! But you shouldn't have waited in the cold.'

'You left me with no choice. I have waited on the Lord to provide me the bone of my bone. For a very long time, I have waited on Him. For two years, He didn't speak. I only heard Him speak a few days prior to my meeting you. I struggled to wait in telling you all that He told me. The words *patience* and *perseverance* kept dropping in my heart. Two hours ago, I wanted to go back home, but He instructed me to wait.'

'I . . . em . . . em,' she stuttered, filled with emotions. 'I will pray over the issue and come back to you. And thank you for coming this far, *just for me.*'

'Just for me?' Temi echoed back the words. He fought back tears. He turned his face away, his eyelid swallowing the little twinkling tears.

It became too heavy for Tenny to stand on the ground. She saw his tears; she saw his resistance. She wanted to be alone. She needed to do some deep thinking.

'Praying over this matter is the key here,' Temi suddenly spoke. 'Seek His face, and He will direct our path.'

'Thank you. I will get back to you.' Tenny hurriedly opened her car door and slid behind the wheel and quietly drove off. He watched as the car disappeared into the foggy weather.

Tenny's brain was doing all sorts of things, ranging from crying, to shouting, to singing, and just all sorts. 'Can this be true? Is God talking to me about Temi? I must see Pastor Lase. I need to talk to Daddy.'

The following day was Saturday, and Teniola drove to her pastor's house as she could not keep the events secret any more.

'Your dreams are self-explanatory. Fruits in a dream means blessing, Teniola,' Pastor Lase told her. 'Blessing is coming your way. God has further confirmed His plans for you through the mouth of this man. It's now up to you to pray for direction on how to run with the vision. I will suggest you go on a day of fasting and praying to authenticate all that you have been shown.'

Teniola went on a day of fasting and praying, but she saw nothing in her dream, not until the following week, when she saw herself and Temi in that same house arranging various fruits.

She reported this dream to her pastor.

'Now, follow your heart. Allow Temi to express himself further,' Pastor Lase advised.

Teniola could not bring herself to call Temi to her office. She was contemplating on how to meet with him when she heard another argument coming from Maria. Immediately she knew Temi was around. Her heart lifted with joy. Something in her was waiting to see him. She rushed to the door and to Maria's office.

'Allow him to come in,' Teniola said.

'He cannot come into your office. He is not a bona fide . . .'

'Oh, for heaven's sake. Why are you so myopic?' Teniola screamed. 'I have now changed my mind! Temi Williams is now allowed to come into my office unscheduled! Get that into your brain, Maria!'

Teniola turned to Temi and gestured to him to take the lead to her office.

'Teniola is the strangest human I have ever worked with,' Maria said. 'She uses her emotions like a remote control, directing me like a robot. One minute she would want to see Temi, the next minute she wouldn't. She needs help,' Maria uttered.

In her office, Teniola apologised for Maria's actions.

'She's fine, she was only acting on instructions,' Temi responded.

'Anyway, never mind, I take responsibility for everything. I am guilty.'

'Says who? My court hadn't charged you guilty.'

'You are funny.'

'You're still in my court, lady.'

'Okay. Where do I stand then?'

'You are not guilty, I say.'

'Yeah. Really?'

'Yes.'

'Ah, that's great. Coming from a judge like you made my day.'

They both laughed and sat on the couch. She was losing words now.

'I'm . . . em . . . I am sorry for the cruel way I have dealt with you. I wasn't sure if God had actually spoken those words to you, not until I had those dreams. And because of the trauma I went through in my previous marriage, it was difficult to just jump into another relationship. I am sorry,' Teniola apologised.

'Oh, Teniola, you don't need to be sorry. The bottom line, I have prayerfully sought for a wife, and now I've found her. Are you now convinced that He spoke to me about you?'

Teniola gave a feeble smile in response. 'Yes.'

'Can we find somewhere more interesting to talk?'

'My office is the only available room except for the conference room.'

'May I take you out for lunch then? Please?'

'Hum . . . um, yes. And why not?'

'Thank you, but before lunch, I have something for you. Please excuse me. I'll be back in a jiffy.' Temi dashed out of her office. He returned and walked past Maria with a bouquet of fresh flowers and some books.

'What am I seeing? Temi Williams with a bouquet of flowers to Teniola's office?' She wriggled in her seat and involuntarily glanced around as though she expected someone or something to pop up suddenly.

'Who is it for?' Maria asked no one in particular. 'This is serious. I will wait to see the end of this.'

Back in Tenny's office, Temi said, 'These flowers are for you, for freshness, newness, and brightness to your beautiful life.' He handed over the flowers to Teniola, whose face was already shrouded with a smile. 'And these three books are to guide us on a godly relationship. I have read them.'

Teniola accepted the books and smiled. 'I have read them too!' she said.

'Have you? Great minds think alike.'

'And for the flowers, thank you. I am still in denial of what is happening. I have never been given fresh flowers by any man before. You are the first. I love flowers.'

Temi loved giving flowers; he regularly gave them to his mum whenever she visits from Nigeria. He noted Tenny's love for flowers and was determined to send some to her every week.

'Flowers are beautiful, they are for freshness.'

He took the flowers and carefully placed them in a long-aged flower vase that looked somewhat forgotten, sitting on the window ledge of Teniola's office.

'I am still in denial of what is happening,' Teniola responded.

'This is real, the Boaz is here!'

'Boaz?' Teniola flinched, as if she'd been stung by a swarm of bees, almost shot up from her chair.

Temi was taken aback by Teniola's frightened expression. 'Boaz is Ruth's husband. He was mentioned in the Bible.'

'I know . . . I know . . . There is a reason for my action.'

He looked down at her, his eyes asking the questions. 'And the reason?'

'We'll talk about that later.'

'Okay, there is a lot to talk about anyway. Shall we leave for lunch now?' Temi asked.

'Oh, yes. Where we are going?'

'Somewhere special.'

As the couple emerged from the office together, Maria marvelled in disbelief. She stared, positively speechless.

'I'm going for lunch,' Teniola announced to Maria.

'You . . . you're going . . . where? With Temi?'

'Yes.' And dropping her keys on the table, Tenny answered, 'Please lock up my office. There are some confidential documents on my table.'

Maria held tightly to the keys as she watched them leave. 'She is weird.'

At the restaurant, after a delicious lunch, Temi narrated how his first marriage failed and how he tried to save the marriage before his ex-wife filed for divorce. Though he had been a Christian, his time of loneliness drew him closer to God.

'On what grounds did your marriage fail?' Tenny asked.

'Irreconcilable differences, my ex-wife claimed, only to discover she was having an extramarital affair.'

'Shame,' Tenny uttered softly. 'I am going through the same divorce process here! My husband, Rob, cheated on me, even flaunting it in my face. Now, he has filed for a divorce on the grounds of irreconcilable differences, just like yours.'

'We have so many things in common, and I believed destiny had brought us together. How do you intend going with the divorce proceeding?' Temi asked.

'I am waiting for the two-year separation to come to effect so that the court can dissolve the marriage. I will not voluntarily sign the divorce documents.'

'It is painful, but God will guide you through. As for me, God had spoken once. Twice I heard him say you are my wife.'

Tenny again marvelled at Temi's staunch confidence in hearing from God. She wondered how Temi found peace in almost everything they had talked about.

'I would like to make a confession.' It was a sudden digression by Temi.

'A confession?' Tenny echoed.

'Yes. I lied to you in Abuja that I did not know when I was returning to the US. Of course, I knew my return date, but when I heard you were leaving the following day, I didn't want to miss the opportunity of chatting with you. I went straight to the airport to buy a new ticket with the airline you were to travel with.'

'That must have cost you a fortune,' Teniola replied.

'Fifteen hundred dollars.'

'And your old ticket?'

'Forfeited,' he said.

'This love *naa wa oo*.' She saluted his courage and doggedness.

'It is an investment that will pay off at the end. I am a businessman.'

She laughed.

They finished their lunch, and Temi dropped Teniola at the entrance gate of her corporation. Before entering her office, she dropped a packed lunch on Maria's table. 'Temi bought you lunch.'

Maria was dumbfounded. 'He what . . . ? Hey . . . what is going on here? You two can not turn me into a raving lunatic! Are you two dating?'

Tenny didn't respond but walked towards her office.

'What's inside the bag anyway?' she murmured as she opened the package. The aroma of roast chicken with piri-piri sauce wafted to Maria's nostrils. 'This is getting irresistible.' She tore open the pack in a hurry. She yanked the chicken thigh into her mouth. 'This Temi guy knows how to bribe! Well, whatever it is, I have forgiven you,' she said.

Tenny found her way back to her office. She met Bimbo sitting on her official chair with her legs crossed on the table.

'How was your lunch?'

'It was good.'

Bimbo rose and strolled towards the window to the flower vase. 'Nice flowers. Temi must have a good sense of impressing a woman,' Bimbo extolled.

Tenny looked curious. 'So how were you privy to this information?'

'I appreciate Maria for keeping me in the sphere, she can't get it wrong,' Bimbo lauded.

'Hum . . . hum . . . Maria?'

'Teniola, I am happy for you. You have chosen well. This must be God recompensing you for all your troubles. Temi is a good man, a man who loves and serves the Lord with all in him. He is successful and extremely humble. You can't ask for more.'

'Now tell me, Bimbo, for the umpteenth time, were you aware of Temi's intention from the start?'

'Nope, he had never discussed anything or asked a single question about you.'

'I'm kinda getting to like him,' Teniola said, rolling her eyeballs.

'Very soon you will fall in love with him.'

Teniola didn't respond.

'How is your relationship with Femi?' Teniola asked, digressing from the subject.

'We are doing well by His grace. Femi is a good man too. He loves the Lord, and that is my number one priority. Once a man loves the Lord, loving his wife comes easily.'

'I think we are getting there now, and we are getting it right,' Teniola responded. 'So has anything changed on our oil well deal?'

'Nope, we are still going to Nigeria once the seller reviews our LOI.'

'That's fine, just keep me posted.'

Both ladies chatted on their newfound relationships.

**Temi's Poem**

Groan no more, my heart
You have prayerfully searched
You have finally found your jewel
The virtuous one
The bone of your bone
The flesh of your flesh
Brave and humble
Courageous and kind
The woman after God's heart
She, I found.

Maria received a parcel for Teniola. When opened, it was a packed lunch meal from Temi.

Teniola was again stunned. She made a call straight to him. 'Thanks for the meal, but you don't have to do this.'

'Then you'll get more!' he answered.

She laughed. 'Thanks, Temi. I really appreciate this.'

'My pleasure. So how has your day been?' They chatted for a while before hanging up the phone.

Temi made it a duty to send scriptural text messages to Teniola each morning and ordered her lunch or picked her up for lunch when opportune.

Week after week, they would go for lunch together, and during one of their lunches, Temi explained that he would be conducting a panel interview with some service providers for his IT business and that his colleague who was meant to conduct the interview with him would not be available. He then asked if Teniola could join him on the panel.

'Which day? What time?' she asked.

'Next Monday, 12 noon at my office.'

'Where is your office?'

'I'll send a driver to pick you up.'

'Is it not surprising that I've never been to your office?'

'Take your time, no rush.'

'Okay. Do I need to review your selection criteria?'

'Yes, I'll forward them to you by email.'

'There is a particular provider who, after we'd shortlisted him for the interview, called yesterday begging me to please accept him for the job. He said this interview would be his last hope, having been unemployed for years. I told him he had to meet all the selection criteria before we could consider him for the contract.'

'That is the best answer. You can't afford to act on someone's emotion,' she replied. They left for their offices.

Monday came, and Teniola was held up in traffic and could not make it to Temi's office until it was the last candidate's turn to be interviewed. This was the candidate that begged Temi for the contract. She settled in quickly, and the candidate was called in. This candidate happened to be Rob, Teniola's estranged husband!

Teniola's seat turned to an ice lake; she could barely feel herself any more. Rob too was shocked to his bones.

Rob looked at her and back at the interview letter addressed to him from Temi's company. He checked to make sure that he wasn't in Tenny Corporation.

'What are you doing here?' Rob asked arrogantly.

'I am part of the interview panel for the contract you are bidding for, so please take a seat,' Teniola answered, firm and very formal.

Rob slowly found his buttocks to a seat and looked strictly at Temi, deliberately avoiding any eye contact with Teniola.

Teniola gestured to Temi to ask all the required questions as she listened and watched. Temi immediately knew what was going on. He interviewed Rob in a professional manner and promised to contact him should his application prove successful.

Rob could not find any other reason for Tenny's presence at his interview other than business affiliation with Temi. He knew Tenny to be totally dedicated to their estranged marriage and her so-called born-again belief, so an extramarital affair was definitely out of the equation. 'We've been separated for a while now. Can she be dating this man? No . . . she's still holding on to the divorce papers, hoping I'll change my mind and come back to her.'

He tried to figure it out. 'But how did she know I was shortlisted for this interview? No, she didn't know, there is no way she could know. I didn't tell anybody. Anyway, whichever way, if I get this contract and report directly to that director—what's his name again?' He glanced at the interview letter, looking for a name. 'Reporting to Temi Williams is all I need.' Rob's riotous mind was asking a thousand questions at a time.

Rob took his leave, tossing a last glance back at Teniola, who couldn't stop looking at him.

The door shut after Rob, and Teniola looked at Temi, saying nothing. She shook her head.

'You've done well, Teniola.' Temi broke the silence.

'That was Rob, my husband.'

'I know. The body language was strong enough to make it evident.'

'So what do you intend doing with his application?' Teniola asked.

'What do you wish I do with him?'

'Do what you think. Is he the right candidate? Has he met your criteria?'

'No, he hasn't. He had no previous experience, and this is a half-million-dollar project we are talking about.'

'I agree with you. He is inexperienced, and his lack of employment these past years has not helped.'

'This is a very sensitive situation here. There is now a conflict of interests based on my relationship with you.'

ABIOLA AWOLOLA

'Choose a suitable candidate then. I don't want him on the job anyway.'

'I can understand your feelings. He's been jobless for a while, did you say?'

'So?'

'I'm thinking of another way out of this.'

'Oookay . . . What do you intend doing then?'

'I'll suggest he start his own business . . .'

'With whose money?'

'Dear, please split from the bitterness. We are in a position to help him for the umpteenth time.'

'We?'

'Help Rob? He won't take it from me. Bring a suggestion.'

'Okay, this is what I'll suggest,' Tenny said. 'I will issue a cheque to Rob to sort himself out whilst you carry on looking for a suitable candidate.'

'All right, if that's convenient for you, we'll go along that line. I could have issued the cheque, but I don't want Rob to think I'm buying you off.'

'No chance! I won't allow you do that,' Teniola interrupted.

A letter was issued to Rob to call Temi's office.


'Thanks for attending the panel interview,' Temi began. 'But unfortunately, you have not met our criteria, so your application was not considered for the contract. However, Tenny Corporation, my business associate, have decided to award you a cash award payment to start up your own business,' Temi explained, handing over a cheque payment issued by Teniola.

Rob was hesitant in receiving the cheque. He eventually took it and looked at the figure. His face lit up in surprise, and then suddenly the brightness fell.

'I cannot accept this cheque,' Rob said. 'I am Teniola's husband. We are walls apart, and I could not find myself loving her again. Maybe I have wronged her, I can't tell.' Rob looked at the figures again. 'Thanks for the cheque, but please return it to her. I cannot accept it.'

'But she's not holding anything against you. Besides, you need this money to start a new life,' Temi persuaded.

'Who are you to her?'

Temi wasted no time in answering Rob's question. 'We are business associates.'

Rob again paused. 'I'm sorry, sir, I cannot accept this money.' Rob took his leave.

Temi said nothing but left for lunch with his newfound love, Teniola Davies.

At the restaurant, Temi placed the cheque on the table.

'He didn't accept it. He believes he has wronged you.'

'The guy is arrogant! If he knew he had wronged me, why didn't he come to apologise all these months?'

'Would you have taken him back?'

'No way, but what I am trying to say is that he is arrogant. He never accepts money from me anyway, nor gives me any, except when he contributed to the cost of my first car. You see, he needs the money now. Why isn't he accepting this money, if not for arrogance?' Teniola answered.

'So what do you intend doing?' Temi asked.

'I'm keeping my money!'

'Okay, case closed. How has your day been?' Temi asked.

'Lonely without you, I am falling in love with you, Temitope Williams.'

'I love you more, Teniola Davies.' They had their lunches and left for the day.

# CHAPTER 9

# Momentum and Rhythm

THE LIGHTWEIGHT JAGUAR XK Touring sports car, with its record of unparalleled exhilarating performance, was eating up the tarred motorway of Bronx County in New York City. The car's aerodynamic sweeping curves and its advanced automotive technology was invigorating. Having reached the turning into Park Avenue, where Tenny lived, the car reduced speed, slowly nosing into the side road. Behind the steering wheel, Temi sat whistling quietly to D'Banj's song of 'Omo yo don make me fall in love.' The air conditioning hummed on, adding to the pleasurable feeling of someone deeply in love.

'Yes, ooo, I am in love,' he belched out from the stomach, making a loud noise in his throat. He changed gear, slightly reducing speed to gain entrance to Tenny's main gate. Once parked, he depressed the electronic knob of his Jaguar XK Touring sports car, and the engine ceased. He eased himself to his feet. Adjusting his shirt and flexing his muscles, he eased out of the car. He walked towards the door and pressed the bell. Tenny, who'd been eagerly waiting for his arrival, shot straight for the door at the first ring. By the door, just before placing her hand on the door latch to open it, she adjusted her outfit and also repacked her hair. The bell rang the second time.

'One minute,' she hollered.

Outside, Temi could hear movement behind the door, and knowing what Tenny was capable of doing, he hollered back, 'Take your time.'

Tenny smiled. Her cheerful reflection appeared in the mirror hung in the doorway. 'I look perfect, this will do,' she whispered. And at long last, she released the latch, pressing down the door handle as she flung the door open.

'Hummm . . . what was going on?' Temi stood still with a curious look on his face.

'Nothing, I'm just getting things sorted.' She fixed her eyes on the fresh flowers which Temi was holding, and he, sensing her inquisitiveness, beat her to the question. 'The flowers are for you.'

'Oh . . . Thanks.' She held the flowers to her nose. 'They smell nice, thank you.'

'So may I come in now?'

'Oh . . . yes, of course. My apologies for keeping you waiting at the door.' She continued, 'You are welcome to my humble abode.'

'Thank you.' Temi strode into the apartment with an air of easiness, observing the environment as he sat on one of the sofas.

Temi loved orderliness. He was a hygiene freak too, but he was not into coercing others into his habits.

'A cute and colourful home,' Temi noted, looking around in admiration.

'Thanks. Our first home—I mean, mine now,' Tenny was smart enough to quickly correct herself, charging the ownership of the apartment to herself.

'After Rob had left, you mean?'

She took her time to answer the question. Slowly, she walked towards a sofa and took her seat directly facing Temi and spoke, 'Rob refused to be part of me in anything, not even after I'd included his name on the purchase of this house. He also trashed the 30 per cent share holdings I allotted to him on Tenny Corporation. He wanted his own. And having done all to make him happy, I take my stand.' Tenny shot to her feet, spinning around in a show of victory.

'Yes, baby girl, you take your stand. There isn't anything else after doing all.'

Tenny took hear seat again. 'Okay, enough of Rob. How was the journey here?' She digressed.

'The smooth mover did sound justice to the tarred motorway, its swiftness was gracious. Overall, it was a smooth journey.'

'It is amazing to watch how such sports cars move faster than the "normal" ones.'

'It's even more amazing how they swallow up a tall guy like me once seated.'

ABIOLA AWOLOLA

'True talk, that is. Anyway, what do I offer you?'

'What delicacy have you prepared for me?' Temi asked.

'Our traditional meal—my favourite, actually—amala and efo riro.' She moved towards the dining area, and she added, 'I am a good cook, you know.'

'Let me be the judge of that,' he teased.

'This delicacy is convincing.'

'The burden of evidence is in the tasting of that efo, so it had better be real good,' he uttered, pointing to the sets of dishes on the table.

'Beyond reasonable doubt, my lord.'

'Okay, present your evidence on the dining table.'

'All set, my lord . . . You may proceed with your evidence gathering. Oh, my goodness!' Tenny burst into laughter. 'This is a serious court drama. I've exhausted all the judicial vocabulary I learnt at university.'

'Life is too short not to have such little dramas once in a while,' Temi responded and moved to the table to have his meal whilst Teniola went back to her seat, watching TV.

After his dinner, he joined Teniola on the sofa, and they engaged in a friendly yet significant chit-chat.

'And your verdict on the food is . . .'

'Discharged and acquitted, the evidence presented was beyond reasonable doubt.' Temi laughed.

'What's funny, and why are you laughing? I am very good with efo riro now, *abi wetin?*'

'I haven't disputed that. In fact, I totally agree with you.'

'So why the laughter then?'

'Well . . . well . . . ,' he stammered. 'I am just happy . . . happy to be here.'

'Okay, I take your word for it.'

Teniola brought out some photo albums of her family, introducing each member. Teniola was the first of three children, the eldest and the only girl.

'My two younger brothers live in Canada—one is a medical doctor, and the other is an architect,' she said.

'Lucrative careers,' Temi answered.

She flipped over the pages of the album, showing her two parents and Pa James.

'This must be your mum, you look so much like her,' Temi said.

'You're correct, she is my mum.'

'Is this your granddad?' Temi asked, pointing to Pa James.

'My biological grandparents are dead. Pa James is my mum's uncle, so he is my granddad. He is a pastor, a prophet in my mum's village.'

'A prophet?'

'He prophesied our meeting. He had already told me that my Boaz was not far off,' Teniola explained, stressing the word *Boaz*.

'He did?'

'He saw Rob leaving me too.'

'Really? What else did he say about us?'

'There is nothing much, apart from his emphasis on digging another well and meeting my Boaz.'

'No wonder you were taken aback when I addressed myself as your Boaz.'

'Yes, you are very correct. The thought of Baba ran through my mind when you mentioned that word. I have been running away from him as I was in love with Rob then, so any thought of getting into another relationship was hitting a brick wall,' she explained.

Teniola then narrated Pa James's trances and all the things he'd said about heaven and hell. She also talked about his one eye, which he closes often even when praying. They both laughed, and Temi talked about himself, his two children, a little about Najite (his ex-wife), and his memorable times with his children. They then talked about things happening around the world, how missionaries are needed in places where Christ was not yet heard.

'It is one of my passions, to reach out to the unsaved,' Temi said. 'I planned on reaching out to the lost souls and the unloved ones. In fact, it is listed in my agenda for this year. I must evangelise,' Temi said.

'Having listened to Pa James's narration of the life beyond, I am now compelled to evangelise,' Teniola added.

'Talking of Pa James,' Temi continued. 'I must see him when I get to Nigeria. I want to hear the end of the story of his journey to the land beyond now that we've finally dug the last well.'

During this visit, Temi was calm as always and very cheerful. He made so many jokes that Teniola couldn't stop laughing. Teniola too, a comedienne in her own right, shared some rib-cracking jokes; they were both choking with laughter.

Late in the evening, Temi prayed before taking his leave. In his prayer, he blessed Tenny, and he further committed into God's care their relationship. They both walked towards Temi's parked car. He thanked her for the hospitality, giving her a light kiss on her cheeks. Teniola wanted more of the kiss; she gently held on to his masculine arms. With both eyes shut, she moved closer to him and wrapped her arms around his neck. Temi remained still, his heart beating faster than before. He hadn't felt like this in a long while—never since Najite, his ex-wife, moved into the spare room before their marriage was officially pronounced as being over. He knew his emotions were running over his sense of reasoning, and he was becoming helpless. Teniola proceeded; she moved her mouth towards Temi's soft lips. She gently placed her supple lips on his. The earth stood still for these two, and the milieu went as silent as a cat. Temi felt a breeze in his head. His body was aroused; his will to withdraw from the one he loved was totally lost. Teniola was caught in between; she longed for a passionate response from him. It was tough for her to pull back now. Suddenly, Temi regained consciousness. He hastily pulled back but held on to Teniola's arms, maintaining a distance between them.

'Teniola,' he called out, the weakness of his voice was made apparent. 'I love you, and you know this in your heart of heart. This is flesh, this is temptation beckoning to us. Let's not fall into it. Let's make our vows known before God and man first.' His voice bore its usual tender tone, and with sombre eyes, he continued, 'Please, let's wait till then.'

Teniola felt rigid and could feel the embarrassment eating through her system. She hurriedly removed her hands from his.

'I am sorry, Temi. I didn't mean to . . . I am sorry,' she faltered, feeling guilty.

'Come on, Teniola, there is no need to apologise. Do you know how I felt when you kissed me? I felt like scooping you up into my arms. Of course, I felt like kissing you so badly. We are both in love, so it is natural for such to happen. But we have applied wisdom, having taken our stand with our righteous God.'

Tenny looked pensive and unconvinced. And Temi, sensing this, added, 'Again my court has not found you guilty.'

Temi's last statement became an antidote, a remedy which charged Tenny to a forceful smile. 'Case dismissed?' She raised her eyebrow.

'Affirmative, case dismissed and finally closed.'

She beamed from ear to ear.

'I'm pleased to see this beautiful face cheerful and blooming again,' Temi replied. 'I will call you once I get home. Please get back into the house.' He gave her a hug. 'I love you, Tenny,' again he pronounced.

'I love you more,' she responded, taking comfort in his embrace. 'And I promise to *behave myself* next time.'

'I promise to behave too. Please go in and have a good night's sleep.' He planted another kiss on her forehead and eased himself into his car. Temi drove home singing a victory song, a song of victory over temptation and over the lust of the flesh. Upon getting home, he called to assure her of his undying love.

# CHAPTER 10

# Fulfilment

THE FOLLOWING MORNING, Tenny's phone clattered, waking her into the new day. She depressed the green button. 'Hello.'

'Hope you had a sound sleep,' the caller said.

'Yeah, who is—oh! Temi, it's you, huh?' And without waiting for an answer, she added, 'I had a nice sleep, thank you. What about you?'

'As ever before, I had a sound, beautiful sleep.'

'What's happening today? Any plans for the evening?'

She paused. 'Temi,' she called, 'please go straight to the point. What are we doing this evening?'

'Dinner at Palm Too restaurant on Second Avenue?'

'Done deal.'

'See you in the evening then,' he answered, and they both hung up the phone.

Three days after, whilst in her office, Teniola received a parcel letter from their oil consultant in Nigeria, informing them of the seller's acceptance of their LOI and attached with relevant documentation relating to the oil block they intended to buy. On this same day, she also received another piece of mail from the family court in America informing her of the dissolution of her marriage to Rob. She was indifferent; she put the divorce papers aside and put a call through to Bimbo to report to her office immediately. She wanted to discuss the oil business. She then called Temi, informing him of the letter.

'Okay, you and Bimbo can go through the contents of the letter, and I will meet with you for lunch where we'll be able to dissect the contents,' he said.

Teniola tendered both letters to Bimbo.

'Congratulations on both, you are now a free woman, free from Rob's bondage. And on the oil well, I congratulate myself too,' Bimbo replied.

'What a relief, the nightmare is now over. Rob can now go ahead and marry his club girl.'

'Wonders shall never end.' Bimbo clapped her two hands. 'Weren't you the crying babe twenty-four months ago?'

'That was long over ever since I fell for Temi. Anyway, please, let's look into the oil letter as Temi will be here by lunch time and he wants us to review the content before he arrives,' Teniola replied.

'Oh . . . oh . . . Temi is now the main man, huh,' Bimbo taunted.

Both ladies did as advised by Temi. They later met at lunch, and they agreed to leave for Nigeria in the next two weeks to view the location of the oil well. Temi followed them back to the office. In Teniola's office, he asked if she would be able to visit him at his house.

'Oh! Yes! And why not?' she cried with excitement.

'Great, and I will get your favourite meal ready,' he added.

'Amala and efo riro? That would be too hard for you. Rice and stew would do.'

'You will be surprised to know I'm a very good cook—a professional one, for that matter,' he bragged. 'My mum used to run a *buka* [cafeteria].'

'Oh yeah?' She giggled. 'Okay, I'll come after church service. Is this why you followed me to my office?' she asked.

'Yeah.'

'I knew something was on your mind when you insisted on coming with us,' Teniola responded.

'Now that you know, I'm taking my leave.' He walked towards Teniola's desk, grabbed a Post-it note, and scribbled something on it.

'Here is my address. Your navigator can direct you. We'll talk again in the evening.' He walked towards the door.

Tenny cleared her throat. 'I have something to tell you.'

He turned away from the door. 'What is it?'

'Nothing serious, I just wanted to inform you that my marriage with Rob is now dissolved. I received the divorce papers today in my office,' she explained.

ABIOLA AWOLOLA

Temi smiled. He stretched out his right hand in a gesture to handshake. 'I am pleased for you. You are now set free,' he said. Now he pointed to the address note. 'Please keep the address, you will need it for Sunday,' he said and left Teniola's office.

That Sunday, Teniola was welcomed with a bouquet of fresh flowers. And surprisingly, Temi's two children, Tiwa and Seun, were there to welcome her.

'Oh! My God, are these your children? They are beautiful!'

'Yes, this is Tiwa and this is Seun.' The older child was a girl of thirteen, and the younger, a boy of eleven. 'They have heard a lot about you and have been longing to know you,' he said.

'I am very pleased to meet you both.' Tenny embraced them.

'Thank you,' they both replied. They were replicas of their father. They helped with her handbag and ushered her into the house. It was a small apartment, similar to Teniola's, but too clean for a man.

'Does anybody live here?' she taunted.

'This is my dwelling, lady!'

'It is beautiful, too sparkling for a man.'

'Well, I live alone, so I don't have anybody to mess it up. My children visit only on weekends.'

She turned to the children. 'You children must be hygiene conscious like your dad.'

They shrugged shoulders and looked at each other, smiling. 'Thank you,' they responded. And they made their way upstairs to their rooms.

'They have a TV upstairs,' Temi added, having noticed Tenny's eyes trailing them as they climbed the stairs.

'Okay, I wondered why the disappearances.'

'I've told them to resume to their rooms upon your arrival.'

'To give us enough room for our usual chit-chat and court room drama?' she said sarcastically.

'Something like that. Please have your seat,' he said, pointing to his all-cream leather sofa. He sat next to her. 'And the journey here?'

'It was all right, the navigator helped.'

He served her some ice-cold drinks with prawn spring rolls. They ate together, telling jokes and jesting on what they had discovered about each other.

'Time for your delicacy,' Temi announced. 'The amala and efo is ready, please come this way.' He marched forward, and Teniola followed him.

At the dining table, Temi uncovered the stainless steel dishes and took from one of them fresh-cooked fish in red pepper sauce, and from the other, the green vegetable stew—efo.

The aroma of the stew filled the room. Teniola's appetite ascended. She offered to serve herself, but Temi insisted. 'This you will do for a very long time. You'd better enjoy my kind gesture now while it lasts.'

'True talk, I'd better enjoy it now,' she said.

He finished dishing for the two of them, and they both ate.

'Are you sure you cooked this meal? This efo beats my cooking,' Teniola asked, looking curious.

'Yes, I cooked it. I told you that I'm a good cook. Wait until we get married,' Temi replied.

'Married!' Teniola echoed in surprise.

Temi ignored her expression. He carried on eating. Teniola asked no further. They both cleared and washed the dishes before resuming to the comfort of the sitting room. They were watching an American movie when Temi slowly dipped his hands into his back pocket and brought out a little box containing a ring. Teniola watched him kneel. He proceeded to hold her left hand, looking intently into her eyes.

'Teniola, the daughter of Mr and Mrs Davies, the granddaughter of Pa James, will you marry me?' Temi asked.

Teniola was definitely caught unaware. She had expected this question long before now, when she realised she was in love with Temi Williams. She loved Temi with everything in her. With Rob, she was always giving, never receiving. But with Temi Williams, it was the opposite. Temi was a pillar of support, an adviser, a counsellor, and a prayer partner. She couldn't afford to lose Temi for anything in the world. She would say yes over and over again on the day when Temi would pop the question. And now he had done it unexpectedly.

ABIOLA AWOLOLA

'Oh! Yes, Temi, I will marry you. I will marry you,' she answered with great joy. Temi slipped the ring on to Teniola's left middle finger. 'This ring is to show my commitment to marry you,' he said.

Teniola too knelt, and they both hugged for some moments. They gently kissed each other, being mindful and in control of the lust of the flesh through their constant prayer. They focused their prayers on remaining chaste and intact for the Lord, vowing to avoid any sexual relations before marriage. They also fasted once each week to pray for their relationship. And it worked; God was in the midst of it all.

'I have waited for so long,' Tenny uttered.

'Have you? I had to wait for your divorce papers to come through.'

'You'd waited? Why?'

'It's good to be organised. I couldn't ask you to marry me when your divorce papers were still pending. I am the man here. I have to make sure we plan it well. The foundation of our relationship must be pure, clean, and godly. So when the storms of life rise against us, we will overcome it by the blood of the Lamb and by the word of our testimony,' he said.

'I need to write a poem,' Teniola replied.

The noble one persisted
He waited for me, having believed in true love
A love that is so pure and sincere
Still in pain from the hurt of the charming one
I walked past the noble one
My fragrance the noble one knows; my fragrance he smelt
He followed me, but I ignored him
I went through waters, the noble one followed me
I went through fire, the noble one followed me
He offered to help, but I rejected his help
I wanted the one called charming
The noble one persisted; he refused to leave
Then wisdom spoke, my very good friend and my companion
He is the Boaz; he has prayerfully searched for you
Embrace him now, wisdom said
I looked back at the noble one, drenched with the waters of my trials

His ever-smiling face beckoned to me
I followed my heart and turned to the noble one
Then I discovered he is not only noble but also charming
He is the true charming prince
I have been recompensed
The Lord gave me double for all my troubles


'May I go upstairs to chat with the children?' Tenny asked.

'Yes. And why not?'

The children had mixed feelings about Tenny because they had never seen another woman with their father; moreover, they had never seen a woman in that house!

Tenny knocked, and Tiwa answered.

'May I come in?'

'Please,' she answered.

Both kids were watching TV. 'Nice seeing you,' she greeted again. 'How are things with you?'

'We are fine. Thanks,' Tiwa answered.

They engaged in small talk and eventually became friends. Towards the end of her visit, Tenny went back downstairs to meet Temi, who was seated waiting for her.

'You are full of patience. I thought you would come and join us up there,' she said.

'I'm allowing you the privacy needed,' he said.

# CHAPTER 11

# Visitation

TWO WEEKS AFTER, the trio travelled to Nigeria. Their first point of contact was the oil well. Temi and Teniola later paid visits firstly to Temi's parents, who accepted Tenny with open arms, and later to Teniola's parents.

'Thank God you are here. Baba has been mentioning your name, he longed to see you,' Phebean, Teniola's mum, said.

'Please meet Temi, my fiancé,' Teniola announced.

'We have heard a lot about you, Temi. You are welcome, please come in.'

After discussion and further exchange of pleasantries, Phebean proposed that they see Pa James the following day.

'Can Temi come with us?' she asked.

'Why not? Baba will be pleased to see him,' she responded.

When Phebean arrived in the village in the company of Temi and Teniola, Pa James was on his resting chair, with both eyes closed but with tears flowing.

'Baba, are you sleeping? And why are you in tears?' Phebean asked.

Pa James didn't respond, but his tears kept flowing.

'Baba, what is it now?' Phebean screamed, obviously losing patience with Pa James's antics.

'I saw Him, I saw Him,' Pa James answered.

'Not again, Baba, you have to get my dad out of your system,' she yelled.

'No, not your father.'

She became more pensive now. 'Who then did you see, Baba?'

'I saw the Lord.'

## Pa James's Revelation

After my passage through the narrow way, I then saw a long wall, very long that I could not fathom its start or end. The wall was also tall, plastered with gold, real beautiful gold. There were no signs of doors or handles on this wall. It was completely flat. I moved towards this wall, and something like a sliding force slid the door open.

I entered and found myself in front of a very big building. The size was indescribable. Written in front of the building was 'Welcome to the *Hall of Salvation.* We shall visit your sin before you can proceed.' There was another door inside this palace, and again the door opened on its own accord, and a voice asked me to come in.

Inside the house, I saw thousands of souls who had come through the narrow way, all shaking and trembling in fear. I walked into their midst and asked why they were trembling. No one answered; they were all terrified, shaking in apprehension. Then I saw an angel, tall enough to reach heaven, beautiful, white like snow, wearing golden apparel.

The angel's gargantuan stature beat my imagination. I could only see up to his waist; he was tall to heaven. His head was stilled up, and he was not perturbed by the petrifying state of the souls. I wanted to talk to him, but the seized environment held me back. The angel's eyes were rounded like balls and massively big. A ray of light beamed from these big rounded eyes, and the heat radiated could be felt in the room.

Suddenly I heard a voice calling from heaven, a very strong voice. Again all souls trembled in apprehension. A particular soul (an old pastor of a church) was called forward, and within a blink of an eye, the pastor's soul appeared before the angel, shaking and trembling. I didn't see this soul shuffle as they had been doing. He just appeared before the angel, and it was a swift reflex action within a micro second.

The angel then read out to the soul, saying, 'You were saved at a year, at a month, at a day, at an hour, at a minute, and at a second, and so we have to visit all your sins committed whilst on earth without repentance.' There was no power to disapprove these dates as all these were correct.

The angel then brought his head down from heaven. His eyes' scanning light trailed him. He then began to scan the soul from head to toe with his searchlights. The light was scorching hot. The pastor's soul then screamed in pain as this light scanned him from head to toe. He cried out, but this angel was not troubled. He continued his search to the end. As he got to the toes, a screen appeared on the right-hand side, and the angel took his eyes off the pastor's soul and looked at the screen.

Then all the sins committed by the pastor whilst on earth without repentance were listed on the screen. The angel read through the screen and made a loud and painful cry, asking the pastor why he did not allow the blood of the Lamb to wash him clean of anger and bitterness before leaving earth. He asked why, during his thirty-six years of serving the Lord, he refused to let go of anger and bitterness.

The pastor pleaded that the devil manipulated his heart to anger. The angel then looked at him and asked the pastor if he would be able to say this to Satan's face. The pastor responded that he could say it to Satan's face. Immediately, Satan appeared. Satan was in the form of a very ugly and disgusting dark creature ever seen, tall and massively built. His mouth appeared filled with blood, with a sharpened carnivorous set of teeth. And the angel asked Satan why he had stopped the pastor from allowing the blood of the Lamb to wash him off from anger.

Then Satan laughed and looked at the pastor. He then said to the pastor to take a look at his clothes, which was in two colours—red on the right side and black on the other side. He then asked if the pastor could tell which clothes he was wearing when the said accusation that Satan stopped him from allowing the Lamb's blood to cleanse him happened.

The pastor could not answer Satan's question. He began to stammer that he could not remember his clothes. Whilst in this dilemma, a loud sound blasted from the angel's voice. '*Depart*,' the angel cried to the pastor's soul.

All of a sudden, a whirlwind from the left rushed into the hall and lifted the pastor far above the ground, dangling him in the air.

The pastor's soul cried out aloud, 'I am doomed, going to hell after thirty-six years of labouring for the Lord.' He cried for mercy. He called on Jesus for help. He called on the Lord for mercy.

But the angel replied, saying, 'Calling on Jesus for mercy here is too late. Such pleading could only happen on earth.'

The pastor's soul looked at the angel sorrowfully, still pleading for mercy. All his pleading was met by another tumultuous wind, which again came from the left. It was a very violent one this time around, filled with venom, spitting anger, and ready to meating him up.

Something extraordinary happened here. Like a tornado, this wind fused with annoyance, straight into the first wind, the merger resonating so fiercely and ferociously. It then began to transform into different forms—one of such was a furious-looking giant, still dangling the pastor's soul in the air, and then it reformed back to an angry wind.

Everywhere it began to shake; the Hall of Salvation reverberated to its foundation from the wind's rocketing bang. The whirlwind now accelerated high to the angel's height in the high heaven (oh my God, it was fearsome), still dangling the pastor's soul. The pastor was helpless. Like a toy in the hand of a little child, he looked feeble and powerless. His cry for mercy became an echo; he was choking.

He once again managed to spread his arms towards the angel for help, but instead, the whirlwind gathered more momentum, ready for speed. Then suddenly, it began to shift, each movement rotating like a fast-moving object. It moved towards the left, and within a wink, it violently whizzed the pastor's soul away to hell. And everywhere went silent afterwards.

The pastor's labour of thirty-six years of serving the Lord ended in hell because of anger and bitterness. Every soul was trembling. I was scared, scared to the bones. *Thirty-six years of serving the Lord ended up in hell because of anger.* Then I began to shiver just like other souls. There was pandemonium in the Hall of Salvation as the next name was about to be called.

All my imagination of passing through the narrow gate straight to heaven faded away. It wasn't that straightforward as *we* thought. There were judgement halls and junctions to pass through.

I was taken away to another judgement room, *the Hall of Restitution*, a room where belongings had to be accounted for. And if any that is not yours was found on you, you will be asked why you didn't return them before leaving earth. Such things as money, clothing, etc. were all accounted for here.

Then another soul was called forward—a pastor again. He served the Lord with all his heart and worked well. But when he had a marriage ceremony for his daughter, he took from the church purse to fund the marriage, even though the church knew about it. When his name was called and he was told that he could not pass through the Hall of Restitution, he asked why, pleading that he had served the Lord with all his heart and might. Why would he not be allowed to pass through the gate?

He was told, 'As a general overseer, you took the Lord's money and did not return the money. And the church just added it as a normal miscellaneous expense for the church.'

The pastor pleaded that he didn't hide it and that the church elders were present.

The angel then asked why he did not return this money before leaving earth. The angel again called out in loud voice, '*Depart*,' and the whirlwind, just like it did to the first pastor, came with such fiery force and whizzed the man away.

Again, I trembled. I remembered all my bad doings, my wife's money which I had taken before. Again, there was uproar in the Hall of Restitution just like in the Hall of Salvation. Every soul shivered in awe of the scorching judgement happening in the Hall of Restitution. After the departure of this pastor to hell, suddenly my name was called. I concluded in my heart that the end had come. I believed I was doomed.

I appeared before the angel at the Hall of Restitution with a rapid force. I stood before him. The angel looked at me, and a video of my life was played before me. And I saw myself returning my wife's money and other things which I had taken that were not mine.

The angel then looked at me and said, 'Congratulations, you may proceed.'

'Proceed!' I repeated, but no one answered as I was again in front of another door, waiting to pass through.

Again I must stress that things were done automatically in the judgment halls. There was orderliness in all judgement rooms. There were no mistakes whatsoever. Many souls that had succeeded passing through the narrow gate might be ordered to depart at any of these gates.

As I proceeded towards the next junction, *the Hall of Unforgivingness*, I met another angel. Just like the other angels, this angel was tall to heaven, beautiful in golden apparel. Written in bold at the top of the hall was 'You cannot enter if you have not forgiven others. You must have forgiven all that offended you before leaving earth.'

This was the hottest and the most brutal hall of judgement, and as with the previous hall, there was no mercy.

The angel called so many names, and I must say, at this junction, many souls went to hell. They lost heaven completely. They word *depart* was pronounced endlessly. Names were called, and then the word *depart* followed. This process was non-stop. Souls were still shivering, crying, and it was so scary, so scary. I again called myself doomed. These were bishops, pastors, evangelists, and deaconesses who missed heaven at this junction.

It was here that they showed me a recap of how my mother made it to heaven. My mother was crying on her way from earth to one of the gates. She was met by an angel who played a recap of her life spent on earth. And before the word *depart* could be pronounced on her, she cried aloud for mercy, asking Jesus to have mercy on her.

Immediately, Jesus appeared from heaven. He descended naked, whipped, and with blood dropping from his wounds. I could not hold myself to behold the body of my Lord, Jesus Christ. It was battered beyond words as each whip cut deeps into his flesh.

On seeing Jesus, my mother cried the more for mercy. She cried aloud, 'Jesus, have mercy on me.'

Jesus then looked at her, still with blood dripping from his body. He then touched her. His blood spread through my mother's body, and within a split second, she was immediately transformed. She was changed and clothed in white apparel, and Jesus too was transformed from the battered body. He was flowing in white/golden apparel, with a golden crown on his head. He stretched out to my mother and held her hands, and they both ascended to heaven.

I watched with opened mouth as they disappeared into the heavens. After I regained consciousness, I then asked the angel how my mother was able to obtain mercy at that junction having been ordered to depart.

ABIOLA AWOLOLA

The angel explained, 'Whilst on earth, on her sickbed, when she was told that she was going to die, she started pleading for mercy right on that bed until death took the last breath. That was why you saw her crying through the narrow gate until she got there. Her last word before her last breath was for Jesus to have mercy on her.'

After this vision, I was asked to proceed to the next gate. I got to another hall, the *Hall of Accountability*. The angel in this hall was just standing there, his face raised to heaven and his arms folded to his chest. I was scared of this angel because he was extremely tall and massively built. I could not even see up to his waist. He wasn't smiling or talking. He just stood there, looking up to heaven.

Inside the hall, souls were giving accounts of all doings on earth with the exact date, year, month, day, week, hour, and second. Again names were called, and voluntarily, souls started confessing all their doings whilst on earth. Whilst this confession was going on, something more sophisticated than the modern-day computer was typing and recording (on its own accord) every word spoken by the soul. All that one had lived to do on earth will be confessed by these souls without anyone asking them to confess.

After the confession, they finished by saying, 'And I died.'

Then the angel looked into the computer that was typing simultaneously, and then a piece of paper flipped out of the computer once the souls had finished their confessions. And the paper automatically wedged itself to a wall, and souls began reading all their confessions. And if anything has been missed out, the soul would voluntarily go back to explain to the angel that there were more confessions to make until everything has been confessed. This was instantaneous, automatic, and in order. I was shivering, scared to the bone about such confession without being asked.

After this confession, a loud voice was then heard from heaven, addressing souls and saying, 'Now turn to the way that's worth all your doings on earth based on your confession.' And these souls looked from left to right and then decided on where to go. So many souls, after confessing to many atrocities, boldly pronounced the way to *hell* as a reward for their doings on earth. And immediately, the word *depart* was pronounced on them, and again the whirlwind from nowhere swept them off their feet and to hell.

Then I moved to the *Hall of Vain Words* (foolish and ungodly talks). In this hall, souls were just saying all the foolish words they have said on earth. These words came out voluntarily. Every vain word that was spoken whilst on earth began coming out of their mouths. They could not control themselves. They would want to stop talking, but the mouth would drop open again, forcefully sending words out. All these words were typed and recorded instantaneously by this same computer seen in previous halls.

And after the talk, if they had repented of this talk whilst on earth and pleaded the blood of Jesus, then blood gushed out from the top of the screen and washed away the foolish talks. Some, after repentance, had then gone back into the world and began the foolish talk, and they died in the process. So the blood only washed the words repented on, and the rest would be left there. As for souls with unwashed foolish talks, the word *depart* was pronounced on them, and they were whizzed to hell.

The next gate was the *Hall of Giving Tithes*. Non-tithers were called robbers. 'They had robbed God, they had robbed heaven' was written on it. Anyone who had robbed God in terms of tithes was automatically ordered to depart to hell. Again the judgement was hot here. Little judgement led so many souls to hell. The word *depart* was heard continuously.

I was later shown an old minister of God who served God diligently. But he was stopped at this gate because whilst on earth, he had a farm, and a fowl had laid eggs on his farm. He had taken the eggs and cooked them not knowing the owner of the fowl. And then he asked why he could not enter the last gate, the beautiful gate. The angel then told him to open his hand, and there he saw the four eggs he'd cooked. The angel asked why he did not look for the owner of the fowl that laid the eggs on his farm. He then began to plead that he was sorry, but because he did not ask for forgiveness, this was counted against him, and he was whizzed to hell.

It was a sorry sight. The old man was lifted up by the whirlwind, weeping like a child for God to have mercy. The most common word here with souls was a plea for mercy. But the angel replied, 'There is no mercy here, depart.' And immediately, the whirlwind whizzed him away.

It was another scary state. I was perplexed. Pastors who had commercialised the gospel were at this junction ordered to depart. Pastors who preached for their financial gains were ordered to depart to hell. It was another fierce judgement. It was hot. So many souls who'd come through fourteen gates were at this junction ordered to depart to hell. I wept and wept. It was horrendous. Hell is *real*; so is heaven. Overall, I went through fifteen gates and halls.

And at the last gate—the fifteenth gate, the biggest gate to heaven—I saw myself clothed in a white garment. All the while, other souls and I were naked. At the front of this last gate, it was written, 'Welcome to the *Palace of the King of Glory.*'

The angel at this gate had so many eyes—eyes at the front, at the back, and inside. The angel was so transparent that you could see things through him. He was tall, clothed in golden apparel. He was very clean and beautiful. His feet were floating, never touching the ground. He was in the clouds with other angels.

He called my name and said, 'Son of the highest God, welcome.'

The door was opened for me, and I saw streets of complete gold with beautiful trees and flowers, glowing and shining. On these trees were beautiful birds and flowers, and as I tried touching them, the flowers opened up and shouted hallelujah. I was ajar. I then saw beautiful stones. Again they opened and shouted hallelujah when I touched them. I did this for quite a while.

Then this gorgeous angel floated towards me and said, 'Follow me.'

And I asked, 'Where else can one go to apart from this beautiful paradise? This is paradise. Please allow me stay in this street of gold where trees, birds, and even stones shout hallelujah.'

'You are in their wilderness. This is not home,' the angel said to me.

'What!' I frisson. 'All these are wilderness?'

Then I began to float with this angel, still within the fifteenth gate. And inside this gate, there were more than one hall, unlike the previous ones. Each hall was called a city.

I then saw the *City of Aborted Children.* These were children that were aborted. Once the child sighted the father or the mother coming, the child would call the other aborted children and announce the presence of his or her parents. Once each of the parents got to these children, the aborted child would shoot forward to ask why he or she was aborted.

Again, confession would start proceeding voluntarily by souls. And if the mother/father had repented of this sin before leaving earth, the child would hug him or her, bid him or her a farewell, and then they would return to their city. But if the parents had not repented, a vision of what the child ought to have been on earth (e.g. doctor or lawyer) would be played to such parent, and the child would again ask why his or her assignment was cut short. And most souls went to hell from the City of Aborted Children.

Then I proceeded with the angel, still floating, to a place called the River of Life. The river was extensively and enormously stretched. It was white and crystal clear, cool and completely clean. I stopped, and without saying a word (but with the intention of lowering down to touch the river), I saw myself being lowered to the level of the river. I then realised that my thoughts were made known. Everything in me was opened and transparent, with nothing hidden!

As I dipped my hands into the River of Life, the waters lifted their voices up in a mighty rush and shouted hallelujah. I moved back and trembled. I dipped my hands again, and the tremendous shouts of hallelujah filled the waters. I marvelled at all that I was seeing. I stayed at this river for a long time, dipping my hands to hear the mighty rush of hallelujah. It was awesome, and it cannot be fathomed by any human.

And the angel was exceptionally patient. He stood afloat, waiting. He said nothing and was not in a hurry to distract me from the precious moment I was having by the River of Life. I could see other angels floating around with souls, giving them a tour on the most beautiful place not to be ever missed. I then remembered, angels are messengers.

After I had finished, we proceeded to another city. It was the called City of the Blood of Jesus Christ. At the entrance of this city, I was asked to open my mouth, and this blood was placed on my lips. Immediately it reached my mouth, and it began to flow into my ears and to every part of

ABIOLA AWOLOLA

my body. This happened again to all souls that came into the City of the Blood of Jesus Christ.

Then I found myself in another city called the City of the Saints. The guiding angel was still floating with me. Here, souls who had passed through all the gates were now called saints. They were countless, all in flowing white garments with crowns on their heads. Some were small crowns, and some were big ones. There were stars on their garments.

The City of the Saints was a very beautiful one. There were horses decorated in golden apparel and in different beautiful colours walking majestically. They were completely different from the horses on earth. The wall of this city was gold in colour.

Then, whilst still floating with this angel, I was taken to see those who *were sleeping* in the Lord. They were all covered from head to toe in shining white crystal apparel. Everything about them glittered. They were all laid neatly in cubicles, sleeping in the Lord. And there were angels, gigantic in stature, passionately guarding and watching over these saints like a mother watches over her babe. These angels, whose heights were tall to heaven, tilted their heads towards these saints, rotating their massive eyes on the saints from head to toe and watching over them. I then asked the guiding angel, 'Whose souls are these?'

'They were those that slept in the Lord,' he responded with patience. 'They had fought the good fight of faith on earth, and having conquered death, they are now resting at the bosom of their maker—the King of Glory. They were allowed to sleep until the day of resurrection when they will rise from their sleep.'

I watched in amazement. What a restful place after going through the chaotic mayhem on earth.

Then we proceeded within the City of the Saints, and I saw countless numbers of angels all crying, 'Holy, holy is the Lord God almighty.' This the angels had been saying from the beginning of the beginning. I then saw another faction of saints rejoicing and dancing to a melodious song of hallelujah. The harmonies that accompanied this song were indescribable. I had never ever heard such ensemble of voices before. It was flawless, clean.

'Whose voices were those?' I directed the question to the angel.

'The angelic voices, they were created to sing His praise, which they would do to the end of time.'

Then as if regaining from unconsciousness, I thoughtfully asked, 'Where is Jesus? I want to see Jesus.'

I found myself floating alone now. I had left the angel behind, and I was looking for Jesus. I hurriedly floated through the saints who were all rejoicing and singing endless hallelujah. Then I saw Him . . . I saw the Lord.

He was seated upon a massive throne. The trail of his garment filled the temple, all crystal white like snow. The temple was endless in size. This Jesus I saw on the throne is different from the worldly imaginary pictures we have of Him on earth. Jesus was tall and handsome. He sat in between the twenty-four elders with a golden crown on his head, and the twenty-four elders knelt before him, laying their crowns at his feet. I watched in astonishment how majestic my Lord was.

Then, He saw me. He rose to his feet and shouted my name in excitement, 'James! James! You made it to heaven! You made it to heaven!'

I ran into His embrace. He lifted me to His arms, looked intently at me, and said, 'Well done, you are a faithful servant.' He rejoiced exceedingly. I could not feel any better; my soul rejoiced in the Lord. I have finally come to my place of rest in Him, at His bosom.

All at once the angels who were already positioned by the musical instruments began to play the hallelujah song, welcoming me to heaven. It was the same hallelujah song that was sang by the precious stones, sang by the birds and by the multitudes of waters. Surprisingly, I did not understand how this came about, but it was the same hallelujah song sang on earth that I heard in heaven.

Then He said to me, 'Go back into the world and give account of all that you have seen. All that you saw must be heard throughout the world. Use books, use tapes, use any informational system to broadcast all that you have seen. Heaven is real, and so is hell.'

I could not say a word.

He now put me down from His arms. 'Go,' He said to me.

ABIOLA AWOLOLA

But I begged not to leave. 'My Lord,' I pleaded, 'this is too beautiful to miss out on. I don't want to go back into that world of sin and death. Please allow me to stay with you.'

But a loud voice came from behind, 'Go.' And an angel held me by my hand and pushed me back into this world.

*　　*　　*

Pa James's eye remained tightly shut, tears flowing without restraint. He suddenly grunted. And with a long low cry expressing misery, he shouted, 'He is here! The Lord is here!'

Within an instant, like a soldier at war, he dismounted swiftly from his seat and held out his two arms in both directions. Temi, who stood by the right-hand side, instantaneously took Pa James's hand, their fingers clasping one another. Pa James was warm from the inside; Temi could feel his warmth. His hands were too warm for a morning. And despite the flurry of wind whizzing in and around the neighbourhood, deep sweat still covered Pa James's head.

The atmosphere became surreal. The heat of the Lord's presence became apparent. The room became charged with His presence. The outside environment wasn't left out; it succumbed to the celestial power of His presence. In preparedness for His magnificent passage, the wind twirled voraciously out into the streets, scattering leaves, piercing through trees, and bringing tall trees down to their knees. All modes of transport disappeared from sight; not a car, bus, or bike was noted. Women and children ran for cover; men scampered in terror. *It was Him*. He passed by in His majesty. No wonder Mount Sinai in the Bible days trembled violently at His presence.

The book of Exodus 19:18 states, 'Mount Sinai was covered with smoke, because the LORD descended on it in fire. The smoke billowed up from it like smoke from a furnace, and the whole mountain trembled violently.'

In the book of Exodus 33:20-23, where Moses insisted on seeing God's presence, God answered Moses, 'You cannot see my face, for no one may see me and live. But there is a place near me where you may stand on a rock. When my glory passes by, I will put you in a cleft in the rock and cover you with my hand until I have passed by. Then I will remove my hand and you will see my back; but my face must not be seen.'

Now imagine His presence in the little town of Gbongan. The ambience was indescribable. His presence was made real—it was awesome, it was overwhelming, it was tremendous, it was remarkable, it was amazing. The descriptions were uncountable because He is the Ageless One.

He is God alone. He is God *all* by Himself. He alone rules. He alone reigns. He reigns in heaven. He reigns on earth. Over many waters, He is the Lord. Over the sea, he is the Lord. Over the land, He is the Lord. He rode over the flood with His chariots. Waters of the earth gathered together to sing His praise. They roar with trembling sounds to sing His praise. No king can command such greatness, except Jesus, our Lord.

The streets of Gbongan could not contain His grandeur. The sun gave up its brightness to the Awesome One; the bright sky suddenly darkened with heavy clouds gripping its power. Thunder, one of His messengers, gave a petrifying sound in response to the call of its Creator.

The book of Exodus 19:15 states, 'On the morning of the third day of the Lord's visit, there was thunder and lightning, with a thick cloud over the mountain, and a very loud trumpet blast. Everyone in the camp trembled.'

As the first thunder struck, the grounds shook, and buildings reverberated. The wind echoed with more force; it was scary. More thunder followed. Streets and markets became totally deserted. Pa James shook uncontrollably; his one eye had turned bloody from his cry.

'He is here!' he screamed all the more.

Pa James began to speak in his spiritual tongue, in a language he himself could not understand—the heavenly language. A personal communication with God. The warmth radiated in Temi; he joined Pa James in speaking the heavenly tongue. He cried out aloud. He wanted to do everything—he wanted to kneel for the King of Glory, he wanted to prostrate for the King of Glory, he wanted to lie down at His feet, he wanted to see Him.

ABIOLA AWOLOLA

He groaned in desperation, 'Lord, I want to see you. I don't want to miss heaven.'

At Pa James's left-hand side were Phebean and Tenny; both were soaked in the awe of His presence. They wept too, calling His name and pleading for mercy—mercy to be counted worthy for the kingdom of God.

Tenny pleaded for forgiveness of sins. 'I don't want to miss heaven, Lord,' she cried. 'Help me, Lord.'

Phebean then took Pa James's other hand and something happened. As if electrocuted, she swung sideways, her full weight yanking Pa James's hand off Temi. Pa James struggled for balance as Phebean was swept into the moving presence of the Lord. She began to speak in spiritual tongues.

'Lord, help me,' she yelled. 'Help me, Lord, I can't do it on my own. I need you to make heaven. Help me, Lord. I cry for mercy. Help me, Lord.' The atmosphere was electric and tense.

Pa James began singing:

I saw someone like a son of man
He was dressed in a shining robe
His head and hair were white like wool
And his eyes like flames of fire
I could not help but to fall flat
Flat at his feet
To behold his face
But I could not behold the face of He
He who has been and He who's to come
Then the son of man moved closer to me
Lifted me up where I fell
He wiped my tears and empowered me
To behold his face
The awesome face of the saviour of the world
The Lion of the tribe of Judah
Root of David
The firstborn from amongst the dead
Go to tell the world, He said to me

That I am who is, who was, and who is to come
I am coming back, and my coming back is very soon
To take with me the chosen
Whose names were written in the Lamb's book of life
Therefore, walk right, live right so that I can call you a faithful servant
Because I am the Alpha and the Omega
The first and the last
The beginning and the end
I am coming back into the world
To take to heaven
The chosen ones.

The trio listened to Pa James's song in silence, with each lyric hitting the centre of their very being, buffing their intellectual ability to reason beyond human aptitude. The lyrics of Pa James's song were polishing their minds about heaven, empowering their vision of the King of Glory in His splendour. Soon, Pa James began rounding up his song, and the room's atmosphere began to get calmer.

After a little while, Pa James opened his one eye. He looked around the room and finally gazed his eye on Temi.

'The servant of the Most High,' he quoted.

Temi bowed in silence.

'I have been waiting to see this day. Are you not the Boaz?' Pa James asked.

Phebean was taken aback. This was the least she expected to hear from Pa James. Yes, Pa James was a prophet, agreed, but this was just too accurate and just too precise.

'Allow me to introduce Temi,' Phebean began.

'Have you not said it, oh, Lord of Heaven? Has it not come to pass?' Pa James interrupted, lifting up his eye towards heaven. 'It came to pass today. I bless this day, oh, Lord, the day I set my eye on the bone and flesh from which Tenny's bone and flesh were formed.' Pa James looked at Temi again.

'As the Lord lives, and by His grace, I am the Boaz.' Temi immediately pulled Tenny to himself, throwing caution to the wind.

ABIOLA AWOLOLA

Tenny could not ask for more. The day marked exactly two years from her last visit to Pa James. Everything started to make sense.

'See you in the next two years,' Pa James had said when bidding her goodbye.

'Your Boaz is not far off.'

'Robert once loved you, he loves you no more . . .'

'He is divorcing you, marrying another woman . . .'

It all came back, each utterance playing back, her brain making some rapid thought patterns!

She giggled. 'The Word of the Lord is true, and it stands forever,' she intoned.

Turning to Tenny, Pa James began, 'Your trial had made you strong. Others are learning from your experience. Going through those heartbreaking moments was not a mistake. God wanted to teach you to hear from Him and also to walk with Him in faith. He wanted you to build up your faith. Having faith in Him is not just a mere word of mouth. Your faith had to be tested, tried, and refined before being approved. And there is a reward for patience and perseverance in the Lord. The reward of your obedience to God is the godly man he destined for you to be with. He knew you cannot cross it alone. He placed with you a destiny helper.' Pa James paused, thinking.

'You have a destiny helper?' He looked at Tenny—a question, not a statement.

'I don't know what you are talking about.'

'Of course, you know. Think, there is a lady assigned with you through the journey to walk with you.'

'A lady?' Temi thought aloud, 'Bimbo!'

'Yes, she is the one. She was assigned to help you through that particular journey.'

'Oh! My God, did she know this?'

'No one knows except destiny. She was destined to weather the storm with you. She was your destiny helper. And in her life too, there is assigned to her a destiny helper to weather the storm of life with her. She had done well, and she is getting a reward from the Lord.'

# CHAPTER 12

# Newness!

UPON THEIR ARRIVAL from Nigeria, Temi's ex-wife dropped the children at Temi's house as prearranged. Tenny was right outside waiting to receive the children as Temi was busy in the office. She wasn't sure of what to expect, but definitely not a fight. Temi had told her much about Najite, how quiet and reserved she was. Both Temi and Najite communicated often, most especially on matters concerning the children. So Temi saw it as a duty to inform Najite—the mother of his two children—of his newfound love, Teniola Davies.

'I left you for another man, it is my loss,' Najite had responded.

The children were the first to alight from the car whilst their mother followed from behind. They ran towards Tenny and jumped into her open arms. There was a tight hug. The throat-clearing sound coming from Najite interrupted the atmosphere.

'I'm still here,' Najite said.

'Oh, sorry, we didn't mean to abandon you in waiting.'

'I am Najite, Temi's ex-wife.'

'I'm very pleased to meet you. I am Teniola Davies . . .' Tenny wasn't sure of how to describe herself.

'Save the struggle, I know who you are.'

'Oh!'

'And I mean no harm.'

'Oh!'

'My children seem to love you,' Najite said.

'I love them too. I've been longing to see them.'

'That's good to hear.' She paused, wanting to say something. 'Um . . . um . . . you've got the best man on your arms . . .'

'Sorry? I mean what do you mean by that?' Tenny choked.

'I am sorry to have embarrassed you. I . . . I . . . ,' she stuttered. 'I just wanted to tell you that . . .' She paused again.

'That what? Please go on.'

'Okay, I'll tell you,' she began. 'Let me tell you something about the treasure in your hands. Temi is the treasure. He is the best man any woman could ever have, the jewel I once had. I am an Igbo lady. I blew my chances with him after being enticed by another man. I was happily married to Temi with everything going well for us as a family, but only God knows why I decided to have an extramarital affair, which eventually led to our divorce. I divorced a man who loved me, a man devoted to his family and to his God. I was definitely out of my mind then, anyone could tell. I could see the pain in his eyes when I moved out of our matrimonial home. He begged and pleaded with me to stay, but like the prodigal son, I heeded not. I was bent on getting married to this other man. Unfortunately, the second marriage became a thorn in my flesh. I wanted to opt out, but by then, Temi was already seeing you. He had waited two years for me to come back. Despite my betrayal of him, he kept in touch. He sends prayer messages and encourages me to keep praying. He doesn't joke with his children, as you must have discovered. I hope I'm not causing you any discomfort with this confession.'

'No. Not at all. Please continue.' Though Tenny had heard the full story from Temi, hearing from Najite sounded somehow more emotional. Temi had told her everything about Najite in good faith.

Najite continued, 'He bought me this car'—pointing to the Chrysler Voyager seven-seater car—'when all that glittered like gold around my present husband turned to copper. Our business went down, and money became a mirage. Surprisingly, Temi, the jewel, picked me up. He helped set up a business, and that was how I bounced back. I cannot but wish Temi well.'

'Um . . . umm.' Tenny was looking for words.

Najite knew Tenny was struggling for words. 'I can tell he's found happiness again. He loves you, he sings your praises. He said God had confirmed you as his wife.'

'He told you that?'

Najite nodded in approval.

'My children can't stop singing your praises too. You've looked after them like your children. I couldn't ask for more. Do you have children?'

'Nope, not yet.'

'Please take good care of Temi, he is a gentleman. My children will continue visiting, please continue with your care of them.'

'I am extremely sorry to hear about the pain in your second marriage. Prayer is the key to everything. I'll advise you to keep praying. And I promise to take care of Temi and our children, they are mine too.'

'Thank you. Temi said you both are getting married soon. When will that be?'

'Ehm . . . I cannot confirm now, but once we've decided on the date, I will let you know.'

'I am wishing you and Temi all the best and a new life together.'

'Thank you, Najite.'

She bid her children goodbye and hopped inside her Chrysler Voyager car, whizzing away.

Tenny stood still for a while, recounting each word that came out of Najite's mouth. Every testimony around Temi had justified him as a good man.

She muttered, 'Obviously, God must have preserved him for me, knowing how my effort in my marriage to Rob yielded no result. It was total abuse, neglect, and rejection. I remember how arrogantly Rob once told me he never gives love and he was not trained to give love! What a demonic and selfish mentality. God, our Creator, is love. How then can a human boast of his unwillingness to give out love?'

Tenny turned and went into the house to meet with the children. Once inside, there was an ecstatic noise as she joined the children in playing around.

'Put things in order. Socks and clothes are to be sleekly folded. Who says that?' Tiwa teased.

'Your dad,' Tenny retorted.

'Get it right, be unhurried to speak, be prompt to think. Who says that?' It was Tenny's turn to impersonate Temi.

'Of course, Daddy!' The children squealed in delight.

They all laughed.

ABIOLA AWOLOLA

'So when is he coming home?' the children asked.

'His ears should be twinkling now after countless mentions of his name. He is joining us at the funfair park.'

'We're going to the funfair, yippee,' Seun, the youngest enthused.

They all huddled into Tenny's sleek Mercedes Benz and stylishly sped off to the park. Temi later joined them, and they spent the day together, after which Tenny returned to her house.

That weekend found Tenny spending the day with Temi and his children. She was there early enough to get them out of bed. After breakfast, they all sat at the table to discuss the wedding.

'Are you two getting married?' Tiwa exclaimed. 'Oh my God, oh my God, I've been waiting for this.' She turned to her brother. 'Our dad is marrying Auntie Tenny.'

Seun looked as if he wasn't part of the humans on earth. 'So what's gonna happen?' he asked.

'What do you mean what's gonna happen? Auntie Tenny will move in with dad and she'll be our stepmother,' Tiwa explained.

'Okay.'

'You asked a question, and you have answered the question yourself!' Temi exclaimed.

'It's excitement,' Tenny explained.

'Okay, your answer is correct, we are getting married. Haven't I waited enough, two whole years now?'

'You have waited long enough. When is this glorious day?'

'This is what we are about to discuss, and I want you both'—he pointed to Tiwa and Seun—'in the discussion.'

'I'm in, Daddy. What do you want us to do?'

'Okay, I'll tell you. To begin with, I need a minute taker. Can you do that?'

In no time, Tiwa appeared with a pen and a paper. 'Go for it, Dad,' she said.

Three months later, the loving couple had their civil marriage at the New York City registry. They proceeded to Nigeria shortly after for the traditional and church wedding ceremony. A week before their journey to Nigeria, Tenny moved all her belongings into Temi's house and rented out her apartment. She stayed with Bimbo for the rest of the week before leaving for the motherland.

All was set for a new life in togetherness. They travelled to Nigeria with an entourage—Temi's two children, ten of his friends, Bimbo and her friends, all the staff of Tenny Corporation (including Maria), staff from Temi's establishments, and Tenny's friends. They arrived in Nigeria on Tuesday and had the traditional wedding done on Thursday and finally the church wedding on Saturday.

At the church service, there were memories that should be logged into the memory bank of life. First of all, Teniola's face transfigured from her usual beauty to a vision of gorgeousness. She actually glowed like a woman who had for months soaked and bathed in Arabian oil of beauty. There was no way one could not adore and appreciate the good works of nature over her. Phebean, her mum, was taken aback in admiration of her daughter's beauty as she walked through the aisle with Dave, Phebean's husband.

Teniola's ebony face was complemented with a delicately created hairstyle, which was crafted by sweeping her hair from her face into an exquisite ponytail, interlaced with light cream pearl beads. Her short stud diamond earrings and thin pearl necklace fitted daintily on her. Her skin appeared softened, radiating with freshness.

She fitted rightly into the Vera Wang designer wedding dress, puffing out her curvy contoured shape. The wedding dress had a slight slit at the front, showing off her beautiful, spotless, hot legs. Her elegant walk was enhanced by the sophisticated handmade shoes. Her ravishing smile captivated all present, even when still under a very transparent veil. Guests stood in wonder of her beauty.

Temi too was immaculately dressed in a two-button grey-coloured Italian tuxedo suit, complemented with cap toe shoes. Bimbo, the chief bridesmaid, also glowed in sequence with Teniola. The bridal entourage beautifully coordinated ensembles simply added to the sheer decadent splendour of the day.

Temi's two children, Tiwa and Seun, were part of the bridal train. Pa James, his wife, Mama, and the parents of the bride and groom were all clad in rich Yoruba traditional regalia, all gleaming in beautiful colours.

ABIOLA AWOLOLA

The bridal train kept marching at a slow pace as the keyboardist hit the music notes.

Temi waited patiently at the altar for his bride. He was asked to open the veil and was left confounded by the exquisite vision of beauty that awaited him.

He blinked momentarily. 'Oh! My God,' he exclaimed. 'Goodness me, what have they done to you? You look stunning.'

The service continued, and within an hour, Temi and Tenny were pronounced husband and wife.

'You may kiss the bride,' the priest said.

The kissing began—it was soft, supple, adoring, passionate, and long.

The priest cleared his throat. 'We are still in the middle of service.'

They gave a momentary pause, looked at each other, and simultaneously engaged in another long kiss. It was a hungry one!

'I give up, these lovebirds are hungry,' the priest said.

What a moment! Applauds and cheers filled the air. The church service ended, and they shot off to the reception. This was attended by guests from far and near.

Music, love, and joy oozed from the beautifully bedecked venue.

Temi sang:

Today, I married the bone of my bone
I married the flesh of my flesh
Teniola, we've found love
And our love is here to stay
I love you.

The wedding ceremony was graced by friends and families who had travelled from various parts of the world, including the UK, US, Canada, and Nigeria. Dignitaries ranged from government officials to film celebrities; even guests all the way from Japan were there as acquaintances of Temi, the man with many business tentacles. It was indeed a memorable day for all present. After speeches, dining, and dancing, the couple left promptly for their honeymoon destination.

In sharp contrast to the merriment, Rob was on the other side of the world, drinking himself away at the Blue Waters Club. He was joined by Clem.

'Wait a minute. Are you aware that Tenny is getting married to a business tycoon today?' Clem asked, turning to Rob, whose eyes were bleary from too much heavy drinking.

'Yes, I heard,' he stuttered.

'And what are you doing about it?'

Rob lifted his eyebrow. 'Doing about it?' he repeated. 'Nothing,' he answered. 'She's cool, man.'

'You've just lost the opportunity of a lifetime, man,' Clem said.

Rob sat, head bowed. He said nothing.

Two weeks later, the couple arrived from their honeymoon, still in the spirit of romance. Tenny charged her cell phone, which had been dead for weeks. They settled in the living room, opening their wedding gifts.

'Dear, please get me a glass of water,' Temi requested.

Tenny's cell phone jangled. Both stared at each other.

'They know we are back! Can't they give us a break?' Tenny groaned. She looked at the screen. It displayed a withheld number.

'Who is it?' Temi asked.

'I don't know, number withheld.'

'You deal with your call, I'll get my water.' Temi dashed into the kitchen.

'Hello,' she answered.

'Congratulations,' she heard the caller say.

She immediately recognised the voice. Her brain was doing a three-sixty-degree turn. She held her breath and paused for a while.

'You're still there, I believe?' The caller asked.

'Um . . . yes . . . I'm still here.' She gathered her thoughts.

'Congratulations,' the caller repeated.

'Thanks, Rob.'

'And I wish you joy in your new life,' Rob uttered and hung up the phone.

Tenny stood still, still holding on to the phone. She stared at nothing.

'Who was it, dear?' Temi hollered from the kitchen.

'It was Rob.'

ABIOLA AWOLOLA

# The Couple's Praise Song

Praise awaits you in Zion (my God)
For you lifted me (space) and anointed my head
Praise awaits you in Zion (my God)
To you alone, my vows fulfilled
Lord, (I praise you) you are my rock
Lord, (I worship you) for you are my redeemer
Lord, (I praise you) you are my rock

When I called on to the Lord
From His temple, He heard my voice
My cry came before Him, into the ears of the Lord

**Bridge**
The earth trembled and quaked
It trembled because my cry came before Him

**Vamp**
He parted the heavens
He reached down from high
He took hold of me
and He drew me out (high), out of many waters

# EPILOGUE

## Pa James

THE FICTIONAL CHARACTER of Pa James in this book is a reflection of the life spent by Pastor Johnson Sulade Adeniji. At the beginning of the writing of this book, Pastor Johnson Sulade Adeniji, in his late eighties, was hail and hearty until Sunday, 2 December 2012, when he passed on to glory.

On this fateful day, he told his visitors to wait in his living room whilst he went into his small prayer room, laid a mat, lay on it, and was swept into glory. This had been his heart's desire for a very long time—to meet his maker. Adieu, Baba.

Lightning Source UK Ltd.
Milton Keynes UK
UKOW05f2159130114

224527UK00001B/4/P